EssexWorks.

For a better quality of life

Mark Simmons

Raider Publishing International

**Essex County
Council Libraries**

ISBN: 1-934360-44-9
Published By Raider Publishing International
www.RaiderPublishing.com
New York London Swansea

Printed in the United States of America and the United Kingdom
By Lightning Source Ltd.

For Margaret

Where is the Home for me,

O Cyprus set in the sea?

Aphrodite's home in the soft sea-foam

Would I could wend to thee.

Euripides

From The Foam Of The Sea

Mark Simmons ℵ

One

He should have been dead. Bull Moore, a soldier of fortune, should have died, in one of those interminable African conflicts, Algeria or the Congo, he had fought in. He should not have been standing in my garage making me uneasy. In eighteen years there had been no word from him and I did not want to see him now, like a ghost rising up from the past.

Even the weather was grey and damp that day, poor for early summer. On such days a garage workshop smells damp and oily. The garage was in a small Dorset Town. Busy in summer with visitors, quiet and deserted in winter. The garage was mine, a back street garage, a one man band, I ran it badly had lost interest in it. I was married too but only just, easy pickings in a way for a visit and proposition from the past.

Under a car supported on a hydraulic ramp, I saw the man walk through the open double doors the paintwork of which was cracked and blistered. He had broad shoulders, his head was supported by a short powerful stocky neck but his face was hidden under the brim of a white panama hat from which rain water dripped, he looked overweight as I was. A navy blue Burberry coat covered most of his body and came down below his knees. The colour of the hat and coat even to my lack of fashion clashed badly, either he had poor colour sense, or did not give a damn.

"Can I help you?"

"Ha! Know that voice anywhere, Mike Harris."

It annoyed me, he knew my name when I was at a loss to place him, perhaps he was from the Inland Revenue that was until I saw his face. Even then I kept a stony expression. He was someone from the past I had no wish to resurrect. His face was tanned the colour of old leather, he must have been abroad for years.

"You don't remember me do you? It's Bull Moore, Cyprus 1956," he said, grinning, his white teeth bared against his tan.

The truth was I was never likely to forget that Mediterranean island or him. It had cost me two toes from my left foot, a mass of scars on the leg between knee and foot, and a permanent limp not so much as you would notice. A few weeks in hospital in Cyprus then back to Malta and discharge from the Royal Marines. The only compensation now a meagre pension, eaten away by inflation. Yet I was lucky, but for that terrorist's grenade I would likely be dead along with the rest of the section, apart that was, from Ginger Taff who broke his leg falling down a ladder on board ship, so like me he never went to Egypt. Funny though, he was dead now, last year he'd fallen down a Cornish Cliff, that man was criminally accident prone but he had paid for it with his life this time.

It had been the Egyptian leader, Colonel Gamal Abdel Nasser, who had put his spoke in with the Suez crisis. The Royal Marine Commando Brigade had been withdrawn from Cyprus only a matter of days after the fighting in the Troodos Mountains that had cost me two toes. Back to Malta they had gone for amphibious training for the assault on Port Said. While clearing the port area adjacent to the canal, Wog Town, my old section got caught in the labyrinth of customs sheds and offices or that's how the yarn went. Cut off from the company for an hour during heavy fighting, Bull Moore emerged the only survivor, so the official report said.

It might have been eighteen years ago but I could still smell that island. A blend of dusty soil, age, and heat born on the Sirocco and Khamsin Winds out of Africa with that reddish sand, there was also no doubt in my mind why Moore was here, this was no social call, for it had been me who found her.

The Marines call it 'thumb up bum mind in neutral'. I had been walking in a daydream not paying attention. My brain had felt on the verge of frying that day while we walked along the bed of a wadi which was nothing but shingle and white smooth pebbles that ranged in size from marbles that could slip you up quicker than any banana skin, to large ones the size of cannon balls. We had been walking like that for hours in the heat of the day which did nothing to improve concentration. Loaded down with packs and radios and a full scale of ammunition, there was not a member of the section who had not fallen over at least twice, tempers were frayed, patience nil.

It was an elbow that tripped me. My main concern as I fell was to protect my rifle sights from damage. For to the infantry man your personal weapon is your best friend, it had nothing to do with the one between your legs, which was not going to save you in a tight spot. The rifle was saved at the expense of skinned knees. I lay sprawled on the ground hot, tired, and in a foul temper.

"Close up," our section commander Corporal Wenmouth, a tall wiry Devon man, said.

"Piss off, Jan. Can't we stop for ten?" I said still lying on the ground exploring my skinned knees.

Wenmouth had gone down onto one knee. He scanned through a complete three hundred and sixty degrees shuffling around on his knee. His brown eyes narrowed against the glare of the sun. He was looking for any tell-tale mark, anything out of the ordinary, sometimes we felt he could sniff out danger. Corporal, affectionately Jan, Wenmouth was a rare commodity, a born soldier. He had saved our national service skins often enough, whether in Cyprus or on a run ashore in the bars and brothels in Malta.

"OK, stand easy, you can smoke," Wenmouth slumped down beside me removing his sweat soaked green beret, "why don't you watch where you're going Mike? You must keep your mind on the job, Jesus, how many times do I have to tell you?"

11

"Do we have to march on marbles and in this heat? It must be one hundred degrees," I said trying to defend myself.

"Yes, and it's the same for them, and they are used to it and they know the ground."

"I don't see the Cyps stumbling along this bloody wadi," said Bull Moore, the Bren Gunner, offering a packet of senior service to Wenmouth and me.

"That's the beauty of it. Its hard going sure, but dead ground, a natural trench, we have less chance of being seen or used as target practice by the Cyps. And we might just catch them with their trousers down."

"What we going to do then Corporal give them a good seeing to?" said Ginger Taff, the radio operator. We all joined in the laughter at Jan's expense.

"Oh you can laugh but it might just work." Jan sounded tired, but his patience knew no bounds, he was always ready to explain time and again, why we did things.

"Tell that to my knees," I added, lighting my senior service from a match Bull cupped in his hand.

It was as I leant forward to reach the match I noticed for the first time just what I had tripped over. It was not a stone, or a root, but shiny yellow metal that glinted in the sun, by this time Bull had seen it too.

"What is it?" he asked.

I did not answer, for I had no idea, but brushed the surface sand and grit away for a better look and feel. There was no doubt it was metal and likely gold for it was soft when scraped with a knife. Wenmouth removed his trenching tool, a short spade, from his marching order and set to work. The rest of the section watched our progress with apathy but no offers of help, for any movement produced rivulets of sweat. Jan used the spade to shift the larger stones while I worked with my hands and Bull used his bayonet. Curiosity got the better of the rest and they moved closer but there was not room for seven of us to work in the confined area. Jan put two on guard while the rest dug. It took us another half hour to uncover a half life-size statue.

12

A golden statue of a naked woman. Gingerly, fearing she might break, we stood her upright and brushed away the remaining sand and dirt. She could not stand unaided as she had no base, but the only damage was to her toes which gave the impression she had been torn from a mounting in a temple or villa. She had the fuller, more realistic, figure of the ancient Greek or Roman sculptures.

The head was tilted to the left, her blank colourless eyes looking heavenward. The expression on her face was as if she was listening. The right leg bearing the weight the left slightly raised as if in the early moments of a step.

"She's not solid," said Jan tapping the cast statue, "but pretty thick all the same, not one of your cheap gold statues."

"Must be worth a fortune all the same," said Stevens the junior member of the section who had been to university and had once been something in the city.

"How do you think she got here?" asked Bull who normally had no time for Stevens.

"Hard to say. But it's certain the river has not always flowed in this direction,"
Jan opened up his map on the ground and traced the wadi with his finger, "the Marathasa Dam here has probably changed the course of the Setrakhos River but it still passes miles from any marked ancient site."

"She must have come from a temple, can't see any ordinary Roman chivvy having a statue like that. Perhaps she was taken inland when raiders were off the coast."

"Doubt she's Roman," added Stevens, "the workmanship is fine, more likely Greek."

"Which means what?" asked Bull.

"Which means she's probably worth quite a bit more, the Romans tended to mass produce stuff, Greek things are better on the whole as far as I know in my limited experience."

"Well lads, that's all very good but what are we going to do with her now?" asked Jan.

"No way do we give her to the Cyps," scowled Bull. He wiped the statues small breasts tenderly with gun cloth.

"No chum, all we will get from them is a thanks very much," said Stevens. His attitude rather surprised me thinking him an upright honest sort for well over a year.

"One thing's for certain, we can't carry her far. And even if we could she can hardly come on patrol with us."

I was interrupted then by the radio crackling into life, which diverted Ginger Taff and Jan away to the 88 radio set.

"You and me found her, Mike,' said Bull, "it's not up to that bastard with the stripes what we do."

"That's sure right," said Jock Orange Kilpatrick, our Scottish Orange man from Glasgow, "she's for the common man ya ken."

All I could say was, "Calm down mate." How Bull was taking credit for the find, at the time I felt was ludicrous, it did not really matter we were all in it together. And as for doing anything without Jan that was out of the question, perhaps it should have made me suspicious then but I thought little of Bull's comments.

"All seven of us have a say, Bull."

"Yes, that's what I meant." Bull was already in the wadi agonizing over the problem, his large head hunched down into his shoulders which gave the impression of him having no neck.

The truth was then, and eighteen years later, I knew very little about Bull Moore. In Cyprus it had only been a month since I had come out from England, fresh from training. Although I had been glad, I had been taken away from a boring job that I had had since leaving school. Joining up had held no fears for me, it was something I welcomed, a means of escape from the hum drum grey existence of nineteen fifties Britain. Jan Wenmouth apart, the rest of the section was national service men. All had been in training with me and Bull.

Paul Moore got the nickname Bull, after the animal, not through any military smartness like bulling his boots to a great shine. It was more in view of his build and fanatical temper which could result in a head down charge. His temper made him an outcast feared by friend and foe with no close friends I knew of. Yet, in a fight, in the mountains against terrorists, or the NAAFI queue in a bar, Bull Moore could be an asset.

"Well, we have two hours to get to the next RV with the rest of the troop," said Jan returning from the radio, his notebook open, concern written across his normally placid features, 'it's not that far but the grounds going to be hard going."

"Don't we know it," said Ginger Taff.

"I wish you sprongs would stop dripping. And we better decide soonest what we are to do with our lady friend before bloody Spencer-Smith comes round the corner and catches us red handed."

Lieutenant Spencer-Smith was our troop commander. Another friendless character, the son of a general disliked by the other officers rightly or wrongly for having influence, and despised by the men for being too willing to risk their lives for his career.

Our seven man commando section was part of a company movement sweeping through the north western corner of the Troodos Mountains on a Cordon and Search operation. The warren of mountain ranges and foot hills was the main hide out of the EOKA terrorists. Less than a mile away from the wadi, in a straight line, lay the flea bitten village of Ayois Epiphonios, the section's rendezvous. The two other sections of our troop were closing in from other directions tightening the net. This movement, or so the military theory went, would seal off any escape for terrorists in the area. The Military Intelligence boys, through their net work of spies and informers, were sure the village was a hot bed of EOKA.

In practice, it often worked out the tip off was either wrong, old and no use, or they just slipped through the large holes in the net. But it was still useful so the propaganda went for us to dominate the ground to show the resolve Britain had. At that particular moment two section B-Company 49 Commando were more interested in the ancient Cypriot we had captured than any terrorists.

"Let's have some ideas then."

"It's not up to you just be'cos of them stripes," began Bull again but he was cut short by Ginger Taff.

"What about that pine plantation up ahead?"

The young pine trees covered a small saddle of land, a ridge, towered over by two craggy cliffs like small mountains.

"We could bury her shallow and come back for her in a day or two," I said.

"Might not be that easy," said Jan, "but let's get cracking. If nobody has any objection in this democratic gathering," he finished looking at Bull who made nothing of it.

Soon, we were being pestered by black flies amid the pines as we dug the shallow grave about three feet deep. It was harder than we had thought. For the simple fact a statue does not bend like a flesh body, and thus required a wider deeper grave.

"How's about a photo?" said Wright, a short stocky Yorkshire man, as we were ready to put her in the ground.

Bull and I held her and Jock Orange Kilpatrick lay in front, while Yorky Wright captured that moment with his Kodak Brownie after which she was quickly covered with dry stony earth. We left the sight unmarked as Jan had the spot well marked on his map.

Still Bull insisted on covering the site further, even when the rest of the section moved off down the hill to the track that skirted around the base of the small hill on which the plantation stood.

For some reason I cannot explain, I was torn between waiting for him and following the others. For a moment, I watched him covering the grave with branches and stones. It was as if he had buried a friend rather than a chunk of metal. But I did not relish the section getting too far ahead and having to run in this heat to catch up. So I left him and still had to work hard to catch up. Bull caught us up as we were resting on a rise from which we had an uninterrupted view to Ayois Epiphonios Village and all the way north to the sparkling sea.

The Royal Marine Brigade had moved to Cyprus from Malta in 1955 and for a year had been engaged in patrols in the Troodos Mountains, internal security they called it. EOKA was our enemy and led a struggle for independence from Britain and its ultimate aim, ENOSIS, Union with Greece.

Down in the coastal towns, the gunmen and bombers mixed with impunity in the crowds, until ready to strike with ambush and booby trap their deadly weapons. After which, escape to the mountains to hide and live off the fear of the simple villagers, few were betrayed or turned away, EOKA was as ruthless with its own people anybody showing any friendship for the British, or had a different view, trod a dangerous path. The terrorists had a mighty ally, the most powerful voice of these people, the Greek Orthodox Church agreed with the struggle for a greater Greece, and claimed the fight a just one for liberty.

Two

Lieutenant Spencer-Smith came from a long line of blue blooded bastards. It might be said in his defence he had been brought up that way so he knew nothing else. In 1914, the male members of his family went over the top armed with swagger sticks while back at headquarters, where there were more Spencer-Smiths, they treated mens lives as mere corpuscles in the grand plan, the bleeding white battles of that war, the war to end all wars. But our Spencer-Smith had had no big wars to prove himself but he still expected to be a General before he retired. To achieve this he had to be ruthless, which went with his heritage, but he also had to use his cunning and brains.

The village of Ayois Epiphonis was quickly cordoned off by the troop. We turned the entire village inside out and upside down, not that they had much anyway. It was the only time in my life I felt like an oppressor.

The village was like countless others in the eastern Mediterranean countries, flat roofed houses with few creature comforts. A tiny Byzantine Church, its icons turned black by the smoke from centuries of candles. The twenty or so villagers were either children or the old but their plight had no effect on Spencer-Smith, he had them herded into the village square which was hard packed earth, the only ornament being a stone drinking trough with a tap and running water, the only one in the village, funnily enough put there by the British Army Engineers. While we carried out the search. Bull and I were one of the search teams.

"What are we looking for in this shit heap," grumbled Bull, "That Spencer-Smith's a bloody fool if you

18

ask me, mate. There's no young people, they scarpered hours ago and taken any weapons with them."

Bull covered me with the Bren gun. My own 303 rifle was under guard, thus leaving my hands free to search, nothing for a terrorist to try and grab while the searcher was distracted. Still it was a job nobody volunteered for, too many had been killed or maimed by booby traps for that.

The older people retained an air of historic dignity. They were resigned to their lot. This was just another bad card life had dealt them. Something more to be tolerated along with the squalor, poor diet, political fanatics of all colours, and back breaking work under the blazing sun.

However, Spencer-Smith was not quite the fool Bull thought. After the village had been searched which turned up nothing, he had us eat and brew up in the square by which time it was late in the afternoon. The rations brought the usual complaints from us while the villagers were kept there watching us indulge in what must have seemed to them a feast fit for a king. While this was going on the villagers were questioned by Nikos, the interpreter, and Spencer-Smith.

Nikos Clerides had a lousy job as far as we were concerned. Hated by the majority of his people and not really trusted by us. I wondered why this clearly intelligent man did it. I came to realise later that Nikos was one of the few Cypriots I ever knew who had at that time the interests of his country this island at heart. He hated the crimes being committed in the name of liberty and freedom by all sides, to him law and order, albeit British, was better than a terrorist war. He knew his course was perilous but he betrayed no emotion.

Spencer-Smith sat at a rough hewn table taken from one of the houses while Clerides stood at his elbow. The officer's blue steel eyes never left the face of those being questioned; once or twice he asked questions in a bored low voice that was until it came to the children. On the table he had made a small pile of sweets and chocolate from the ration packs and then smiled as the ragamuffin children came before him one by one. His smile was sinful and the children so pathetic. For a bar of Dairy Milk Chocolate, a little boy of seven or eight told of nocturnal comings and goings along a track that led down from the mountains. It might have been his own brother he had told Spencer-Smith about, not that he knew the implications, he was just hungry. When he had finished he up turned the table letting the sweets fall to the ground and walked through them, behind him the children fell upon the earth fighting for what was on the ground.

Next, we herded all the people into one of the larger houses and our section was detailed to guard them and the village. All of which was bordering on the illegal, but Spencer-Smith had no interest in winning hearts and minds, just the score of dead terrorists. Our troop sergeant, Glover a small man with boundless energy, had lost too many battles with the troop commander to raise any objections. But he made sure the house was big enough for all the people and they had plenty of water.

At dusk, leaving their marching orders with us, one and three sections set out to lay an ambush on the track, while we continued guarding the village. Seldom have I felt as lonely as I did that night when the rest of the troop marched away, I suspect the rest felt the same for there was safety in numbers.

"You know, Sarge," said Jan to Glover, "he's doing the wrong thing dividing his force like this."

Glover nodded his agreement; it was as much as he could do in front of us. "You're in radio contact; don't hesitate to ask for help. I don't know what's in his head he may be using you as bait. Anyway," he said jerking his thumb over his shoulder, "you have twenty odd hostages," and with that he was gone, with the rest of the troop.

Once the sun was gone behind the mountains it got cold quickly, even the cicadas did not venture this high to sing their nightly chorus. We occupied another smaller house from which we could cover the larger house and the main path entering the village on which we trained the Bren gun. Two on duty while the others rested. Early in the evening I found it hard to sleep though it had been a long hard day.

"How much do you think she's worth then?" said Bull who sat beside me our backs resting against the wall.

"Should be a fortune but there's a problem there."

"What's that mate?" asked Bull, offering the senior service again, I had never seen him quite so willing to share his smokes, and senior service good smokes not woodbines or the like come to that.

"Where are we going to find a buyer?"

"Easy," grinned Bull, "plenty of crooks down in Nicosia, mainly among the Turks, those wogs will buy and sell anything. We just leave the little lady where she is until we've struck the deal."

"You won't get much of a price that way," said Ginger Taff.

"Well, you got a better idea?"

"What about a museum. Bet the Yanks would pay a fortune."

"That's a fact," broke in Jock Orange, "those American's got everything."

"No way, that's the way we would end up in prison," laughed Bull.

"It would be better if you two got your heads down," interrupted Jan.

"Why the hell should we?" Bull snapped.

Jan shrugged his shoulders, "No reason except I think it's going to be a long night."

That was enough for me; Jan had been right so many times before I took his advice and climbed into my sleeping bag. Bull tried to keep the conversation going but my short answers soon made him give up. Through most of the night we heard nothing but for a regular radio check from the troop. It was still dark when Jan woke me from a restless sleep with his boot.

"Come on, sleeping beauty, you've got the dogwatch."

I got up stiff from the cold floor. Outside the sky was just beginning to lighten a pink tinge in the east. The mountain air was bracing as I yawned and rubbed the sleep from my eyes.

"Come on, mate, do you want tea in bed?" said Bull, seemingly as fresh as if he had slept fully eight hours.

"Heard anything from the troop yet?" I asked Jan.

"No, just regular radio checks, but my guess is if anything is going to happen it will be in the next two hours. And that's why I'm going to keep you sprongs company."

"You must be barmy. Get your head down, mate, they won't hit us while Spencer-Smith's wandering around the countryside," advised Bull.

"You might be right. But," Jan screwed up his face, "I have a feeling something is going to happen I can smell it."

Our mates in one and three sections spent a colder night, without sleeping bags, up above us covering the approaches to the village. Things were turning now from black to grey which was greeted with the rattle of automatic fire and the crackle on the radio, 'contact contact' was the only message.

"Stand to, stand to," I shouted and planted some well placed size ten boots on various parts of the anatomy of our four sleeping comrades. They were quickly up struggling into their equipment.

Then we waited. The gunfire continued briefly and finished with the 'crump' of something larger like a grenade. And still we waited for something to happen in all-round defence trying to cover all the approaches.

At last the radio crackled into life. Jan and Ginger Taff huddled together listening to the message. Jan soon had his map out illuminated by a torch. A 'Roger out' from Ginger Taff and the message was over.

"Blimey Jan, he's put us right in the firing line," said Ginger Taff, but Jan took no notice.

"Right lads, fighting order only. We are going to sweep through to the other section's position. The idea is to try and drive the Cyps back up the defile. The password is Pink Balloon; don't forget it I don't want anybody shot by our mates, Pink Balloon."

"Bloody walking target," said Bull.

We all knew just how bad our position was. For some reason the villagers as bait idea had been dropped by Spencer-Smith, and all of the troops' marching orders were to be left unguarded, it was obvious Two Section were the bait now.

We left the village in arrow head formation with Jan taking the point. The terrain was rocky and not ideally suited to the arrow head, but single file or extended line would have made us too easy a target. Even so with the rising sun at our backs we were rapidly being silhouetted but to rush blindly up there was equally as dangerous we took it slowly.

Three times within barely an hour, Jan stopped us and went to ground and we lay there listening. I could hear nothing above my own breathing and remember thinking, "I must give up the cigs."

We had only been three miles apart, but in many ways it might just as well have been thirty. Yet it was an enforced stop made by another radio message that caught us out.

"Jesus, Spencer- Smith wants us to get a move on," said Ginger forcing us to stop again.

We were a mile from the village in scrub-land dotted with a few poor trees that clung to the thin stony soil at drunken angles. It was then we came under fire.

"Take cover!" shouted pretty well everybody in the section and we all went to ground.

Later, I found out there were only three of them armed with a sten gun, an ancient rifle and one grenade. My wounding in a way was my own fault. My cover was bad and I had no idea where the enemy were. Even Jan's shouted fire control orders made no sense to me. But a few yards to my front was the remains of a low terrace wall which was the main culprit in blocking my vision. Their shooting was high and I was comforted by the steady bursts Bull was firing from the bren gun. He was a good gunner and would not merely blast away at nothing. I took the risk that he was keeping them pinned down and I moved forward toward the wall.

The shrapnel from the 36 grenade caught my left foot right under the boot, a split seconds difference and it would have been between the legs which looking back on it makes me cringe even now. If I had stayed where I was I would have been alright. Bull cut down the EOKA man fractions of a second after he threw the grenade. By the time the shrapnel reached me most of the force of the explosion was spent but it still spun me around like a top, and then I hit the ground hard for the second time in twenty-four hours. I felt no pain rather disbelief that I had been hit. In a state of shock I watched fascinated as a dark red stain spread across my lower trouser leg and began running from my boot.

"Contact, contact. This is B under fire, one casualty."

I could hear Ginger Taff yelling into the radio, and Jock Orange was nearby cursing some strange Celtic oath at the top of his voice. I remember thinking, "Taff, you should be speaking 'clearly and with pauses' not shouting," that's how we had been trained.

We had soon won the fire fight or more likely with one of them dead the other two broke off the action and melted away. By which time I had passed out through loss of blood and shock.

They carried me back to the village on a stretcher made of capes. The medic soon had me on morphine and things descended to a garbled dream it only wore off after surgery in the military hospital Akrotiri. I never saw any of the section again until about a year before Bull Moore walked into my garage.

Three

My next memory was of being closeted in the antiseptic pristine efficiency of the military hospital, Akrotiri. But as my memory came back, fear came with it. My legs were covered by sheets laid over a wire tunnel like contraption to keep the weight off them. I flung back the sheets. Both legs were still there, although the left was bandaged to the knee. The relief was intense flooding through my body. Then I began to doubt my own eyes and started on the bandages. Stupid really I could feel the leg underneath and my foot. But had I read somewhere you could still feel the limb even after amputation, it was all psychological.

"Young man. Just what do you think you are doing?"

She swept toward me like a pristine battleship at full speed. The bandages were replaced, not that I had got very far, and the bed made, with me in it including hospital corners.

"Nurse, what about my leg?" I pleaded.

"Nurse! Young man. Nurse!" she boomed, "I am a Sister. This is my ward and you, Marine Harris, are a patient and you will behave."

There was no answer to that. She had more presence than any Sergeant Major I had known. She was big and buxom, in her forties, but later I found out with a big heart to match.

"The doctor will be doing his rounds in an hour," she leant close to me to adjust my pillows. She smelt of antiseptic, "Two small toes off the left foot, some scarring on the same leg, a few weeks and you will be back in Blighty," she whispered.

In days, bullied by the Sister, I was on my feet, albeit on crutches. But I felt lonely left behind knowing the Commando Brigade had pulled out, and later would spearhead the attack on Port Said in Egypt. My oppos were going to war, but that was all in the future. All that was left for me was to get home as quickly as possible for demob. The RAF Doctor had said the only way I might stay on was to become a regular and sign on for twelve years, after all the mob hated sending home national servicemen with bits missing, they had to pay them for life, but he was still doubtful they would take me. But it was only wishful thinking really, for soldiering did not have sufficient appeal to me to commit my future to it.

It was a surprise when Nikos Clerides came to visit me. He was obviously uncomfortable about it and the Sister was equally suspicious of Clerides. She watched us from the end of the ward like an eagle, albeit a big one.

"How's the leg, Marine Harris?" he began.

"Call me Mike, Clerides, its good of you to come and visit me. You must be busy."

His sad eyes rested on me for what seemed an eternity. I was at a loss to make conversation; I knew nothing about the man, in the end I had to look away. What on earth could he want?

"I have lost two toes," I said just for something to say, "could have been worse might have been the leg, or my life," I smiled trying to be light hearted looking back into his inscrutable face.

"Your friends in the Two Section had to leave in a hurry you know," he glanced up the ward to see the Sister was writing at her desk, at last satisfied that Clerides was not going to run amuck. He turned back to me and continued in a lowered voice, 'they left a letter for you with me. But told me not to bring it here you must collect it from me. Why should they do this, Mike?"

"Blow me, mate. No idea, all a bit secretive," I said jokingly, knowing more than likely it had something to do with the statue.

"Well you can collect it from my Taverna at Curion beach."

"Sure Clerides, I will be up and about soon due some sick leave before they ship me home. Good of you to let me know." After a few pleasantries, Clerides was gone.

In ten days, I was granted a week's sick leave which looked like it would be a bit of a bore, the only marine in a largely deserted RAF transit barracks. Collecting the letter was the only thing I had to do. It never occurred to me it might be an EOKA trap, not with Clerides, no, not with him. With a lift in an army truck I got down to Curion beach it was not off limits and had a regular armed patrol.

Clerides' beach taverna was no more than a shack, with some bamboo shades and a handful of wooden tables and chairs. There were a few people down on the beach but the taverna appeared deserted.

I sat down; it was early I would wait a while. Perhaps take a swim in the inviting blue green water.

"Kalispera, can I help you?"

She took me completely by surprise. She had not emerged behind the bar but approached the taverna from the route I had taken. She had hardly made a sound crossing the sandy soil. She smelt like fresh scented air even in the growing heat. She stood her arms folded defensively across her chest. The impression was she did not quite trust me, an attitude I had come across before in the Cypriot people, but they would never be rude to a stranger. Her eyes I will never forget, they were dark brown with an intensity that seemed to penetrate your soul.

"Have you been on the island long?" she asked, moving behind the bar.

"About a month."

Her air of confidence and beauty made me uncomfortable. She had the complexion of a local, but her voice betrayed little accent. Her hair black and long, but in a curiously old fashioned way was loosely plaited which

27

partly revealed a slender neck. Her nose was long and her eyes dark with a curious hint of oriental slant. She wore no make up, I doubted she was twenty but her manner made her seem older.

"Can I get you anything?"

"Yes, a Keo beer please, and also I came for a letter Clerides is holding for me, I'm Mike Harris"

"Oh, the mysterious Mr Harris with strange letters."

"Well, nothing very mysterious about me just one of your plain old boring blokes."

I could have kicked myself; it was hardly a good chat-up-line. She brought the beer and then disappeared into the shack. Returning, she placed the letter before me and then disappeared again. I had wanted her to stay but felt unable to ask her. But still, the letter's contents were a little mysterious, but soon left me flat after a few words. They did not even ask how I was. It merely stated the statue was still under the soil in the plantation; we would all meet in Malta as soon as possible, and was signed by Bull Moore.

"So, you don't trust me, and how am I going to get to Malta?" I said out loud.

For a moment I thought of trying to recover it myself, but the obstacles soon mounted. I had no map of the exact location, the whole area was crawling with EOKA, I was alone no I dismissed it from my mind. Why did Bull have to be so secretive? Why make Clerides come to the hospital in that manner? It could put him in real peril. I shook my head, it did not matter now. I was going home in a few days, so the letter I destroyed, ripping it into small pieces.

"Was it bad news?" asked the girl close beside me. I had the idea she had been watching me.

"No, not really, it just doesn't really matter any more." Plucking up courage I asked her to join me in a drink.

She thought for a moment a smile lighting up her face, which at that moment appeared almost eastern, with that kind of slant to her eyes, "Yes, why not, for I think you are a little sad."

28

"Sad, oh I don't know, perhaps it's because I must go home soon."

"Going home to your loved ones should be a time of joy. But have you seen much of our island?"

"Only a few villages in the Troodos."

"Ah well, we can put an end to that. Come,' she stood, 'I will take you back in time, up there,' she stood and pointed to the cliffs behind the beach, 'Ancient Kourion is up there. You will come with me, Mike Harris. But first, I am Eleni we must shake,' she said offering me her hand which was cool but the grip was tight.

She must have read the hesitation on my face. Some soldiers had ended their days trusting a pretty face. Even nearby, at RAF Akrotiri, a sergeant had been killed by a Cypriot workman asking for a drink of water, shot in the back of the head while fetching it. People were dragged from cars on remote roads to be executed; soldiers were gunned down in the streets in broad daylight. And how did she know my name, well that was easy it had been written on the letter in Bull's large childish printing. How did I know she was Clerides' daughter, he had never mentioned a daughter before not that he had spoken to me much anyway.

"Oh, you soldiers trust no one,' her eyes flared with the anger of her retort. "I am Eleni Clerides, my father you know. He works for the British at great personal risk. My mother was English she came from Kent," that remark explained a lot, "it is the garden of England you know. I am not EOKA."

"All right, all right," I held up my hands in submission, "we live with mistrust so it becomes a way of life and a way to survive."

"I will forgive you this time but trust me. Love is more powerful than fear. Jesus taught us in the scriptures to love one another."

Well I was all for that as far as she was concerned. But whether her definition of love was quite what I had in mind was another thing.

Although the cliffs behind the beach were nothing like sheer and no more than a mile away, my foot was still in no condition for scrabbling up cliffs. But Eleni soon wheeled into view an old BSA an M20 of World War Two vintage motor bike, ex service still in its olive drab paint. She started it expertly on the kick start and the engine beat was strong and steady. I climbed on behind her.

"Hold on tight," said Eleni, laughing as she let in the clutch.

My arms were around her waist as we gathered speed. Her hair was around my face, it felt silky and smelt fresh. Against my arms I could feel the rise and fall of her breasts under her thin white blouse.

The ride was all too soon over and we spent the next two hours clambering over the ancient stones of the scattered site of Kourion. Eleni told me the place had been inhabited since Neolithic times although most of the remains belonged to the Greek-Roman periods, which was rather wasted on me. I was rather more interested in watching her but I was swept along with her in her enthusiasm for the subject.

The cool of the morning had gone by the time we reached the theatre, whose row upon row of stone seats could seat thousands. Here we sat in the shade for some rest. I was sweating heavily; two weeks mostly in bed had not done much for my fitness. We drank water from a bottle Eleni had brought with her and gazed at the sea two miles below.

"You know I come here often but mostly alone."

"It's a beautiful place," I nodded.

"Yes, but it's more than that,' she hesitated looking for words, "the past seems to reach out to me. To give me it's peace away from our dirty, petty violent world."

"Oh, I suppose they had their troubles too."

"Yes, you are right. Like so many things it is only an illusion."

Part of me felt sorry for this girl, being part British part Cypriot must be about the worst combination on the island. No wonder the past appealed, it was a safer means of escape.

"Well," she said, breaking my chain of thought, "we better get back to the present and ready for the lunch time rush."

The lunch time rush consisted of about half a dozen service men that had come for a swim and a quiet drink, away from the barracks and lying on your bunk reading. And I suspected a few wanted a look at this strange, beautiful, Cypriot girl. It made me feel guilty for not having trusted her earlier.

Clerides arrived on an even more ancient motor bike. He greeted his daughter with a peck on the cheek. They talked in Greek and his blank eyes came to rest on me, as if saying what are you doing here. I was forced to look away from his stare.

I spent nearly all my leave with Eleni. It was not arranged so, there was no real date about it. I just turned up at the taverna and off we would go. For the lunch period she would return to help her father. It was not even that we could go all that far because of the restrictions on movement on the island.

We spent a lot of time at the ruins of Kurion. We wandered along the coastline and swam naked at a remote tiny rocky cove in the clear warm sea. She seemed unconcerned about her body or mine come to that, perhaps she thought the cove hard for anybody else to stumble across. We had little physical contact; we held hands a little and kissed a little.

Two or three days into my leave, Clerides sent Eleni off on an errand, he opened two bottles of beer when she had gone and passed one to me.

"Mike, she is young as you are. She is Cypriot, better she marries one of her own. It has cost her much having an English Mother; an English husband would mean leaving Cyprus at this time. Perhaps forever. Could you see her doing this? No," he shook his head sadly, "she loves the very stones of this land."

He was then distracted by a customer. I had no reply, perhaps he was reading too much into it, all I could do was stare at the beer in the glass and the condensation running down the sides.

It was late on the fourth day the last time I saw Eleni. We were dressing after our bodies had dried in the sun from a swim. From far off in the distance above the mountains came a rumble of thunder. Eleni seemed to listen intensely to this a sad look crossed her face.

"Yes, I know," she said in a whisper, but the remark was clearly not addressed to me. Then she smiled as if for my benefit, "Sorry, I'm thinking aloud."

"Don't worry, I do it all the time,' I said trying to lighten the atmosphere. It had not been the first time this sadness came between us.

She dropped me at the hospital, drawing admiring glances from the sentry at the gates, and promised to see me at the taverna the next day. It would be my last day and she told me we would do something special. I looked forward to that but dreaded our parting.

On that last day I found the taverna deserted, no sight of Eleni or her father. I hung around all day on the beach I asked some of the guys from the base, they all knew who I was talking about but had no idea where they were or where they lived.

Eleni's words came back to me about trusting people and here she was letting me down. "Just like all the tarts," I muttered, but I knew that was not true.

I felt devastated when at dusk I made my way back to camp, there was nothing else I could do.

In my mind I blamed Clerides, he had stopped her. Perhaps I should have been stronger, not taken the plane home stayed on the island and looked for Eleni. I could have written, but somehow that did not feel right and anyway, where would I have written to? The taverna on Curion beach? But if I was to return to Cyprus would she still be there? After eighteen years, I wondered what cards life might have dealt her what fate might have in store.

Four

Bull had lost most of his hair, unlike me, mine had gone grey. He was thicker set but just as powerful as his handshake proved.

"How are you, Bull, it must be what, almost twenty years?"

"Eighteen to be exact, mate."

I knew as well as him how long it had been and knew why he was standing in my garage. But I was not going to let on I knew why he was there. The crunch of gravel distracted us as a car drew up. The bonnet of Joeanna's red Alfa Romeo Spider 1750 appeared outside the up and over doors. That was all I needed, she would want to know the ins and outs of everything.

"That's the wife just arrived, Bull. Do you want a cup of tea?" I said ushering him toward the office which barely fitted the description.

It was more a store room and none too tidy, which contained the phone, tea things, years of paperwork, shelves of manuals and parts, two battered armchairs and a settee used for a few hours sleep on all night jobs, not that there had been many of them lately, it had been more a refuge from Joeanna. But she was in the office today by the side door, unusual for her, such places being below her.

Joeanna had been a real looker ten years ago, but her narrow angular face did not help conceal the age lines that were creeping up on her. It would not have been a problem in somebody not quite so vain. However, she was skilled in the application of make up and a had a good trim figure, although she was a bit flat chested she could still turn men's heads.

"Joeanna, this is Bull Moore an old friend from my days in the Royal Marines. Bull, this is the Mrs," I said, knowing calling her the Mrs annoyed her.

They shook hands and were obviously both impressed as they drank each other in, people who looked after their bodies, vain the pair of them. Depression rising I turned to the tea things.

"Well, you have done well for yourself, a garage, and a bird like this."

Joeanna giggled. If I had called her a bird the verbal attack would have been whip like.

"You're not really called Bull are you?"

"No, that's his nickname," I butted in. Joeanna could have talked for England, 'Look I'm busy at the moment, bit of a rush job,' I continued handing out the tea in mugs, "what is this Bull, just a social call?"

"Don't be so rude, you're real grumpy today, Mike," she said poking her tongue out at me.

Bull reached inside his jacket pocket and passed me an old photograph. It was a black and white that had turned brown at the edges with age.

"Remember that?" he said.

It showed six grinning young Marines beside and holding the golden statue.

"Come on, let's have a look," protested Joeanna. I handed her the photograph, "Is that you?" she laughed, "my my, how young you all were. How times have changed."

"I'm not likely to forget that island, Bull, I was damn near blown to bits on it. I just hope you are joking," but I knew he was not. Not only by the determined look on his face but by the mere fact that he stood in my garage.

"What are you holding, Mike?" said Joeanna holding the photograph up to the window, "looks like a naked girl or child. What were you up to, is she dead or something?"

"Oh yes, she's dead alright and been that way more than a thousand years," I said.

"In fact more like two thousand five hundred, Mike," said Bull.

"She may not even be there still. And even if she was, how would we get her out?" I was already trying to find obstacles to any venture.

"Look, this needs a lot of explaining," broke in Joeanna finding her tongue again. I could tell already this was going to run and run and groaned inwardly.

"Why not come to dinner tonight at about seven," offered Joeanna.

"Thanks very much you two, I'll bring some wine. I know where you live," with that remark he hurried from the office.

"Why did you do that, you stupid cow?" I said furious with Joeanna.

"Because you were just going to send him packing and Mr Bull and his story sounds interesting. And anyway you never tell me anything about your military exploits."

"That's the first time I remember anybody calling Bull Moore interesting, lethal might be a better word. Anyway too late now, what did you want?"

"I thought you could give the Alfa a wash instead of sitting around doing nothing."

"Wash it yourself," I said storming out of the office slamming the door behind me.

Her laughter followed me as I walked across the workshop. The rest of the day passed with a series of questions I asked myself. None of which seemed to have an answer and just lead in circles. How had Bull found me? How had he survived the ambush in Suez in 1956 when the rest had died? They were all dead now. Just the two of us left. Why did he need me now? Would the statue still be there? How would we get it out of Cyprus and then sell it? And would it even be right to try, we would be no better than grave robbers. If I was honest that last one did not bother me all that much, grave robbing had gone on for centuries, and been the vocation of many prominent people.

Then there was Eleni, was she still alive and if so what sort of life had she led. I tried not to think of her she would be just an added complication and perhaps better left in the past.

By the time I drove home in my ageing Ex-Post Office Morris Minor van my frame of mind had much improved. Home was a semi detached house built just after World War II in what might now be called a good area of the town. For once, Joeanna was home before me. Her red Alfa blocked the drive which was just her way of trying to get under my skin, but my mood was too good then. So I just moved it to get the van in of the road.

That night, I was determined she would see a different me which would be more like the old days. No way would she be running this show.

Bull arrived by taxi, on time, carrying a carrier bag of wine and brandy. The meal, for which Joeanna had made a real effort, passed largely in silence save for the usual pleasantries which was an improvement on most of our meals. Bull drank little I noticed but was quick to fill our glasses. After the meal, the dishes were consigned to the kitchen sink while we returned to the comfort of the lounge for coffee and brandy.

There Bull took over the large coffee table, glasses and cups were left on the floor or mantelpiece above the fireplace, and he emptied the contents of a large folder on the table. Maps, a stack of photographs and several large glossy books were most of the contents. Joeanna was quickly flicking through one of the books which appeared to be a museum guide.

"Well, come on then Bull, give us your sales pitch," I said leaning back into my armchair. Bull sat in another chair while Joeanna was on the settee with her feet tucked under her bottom.

Bull picked the photo he had shown us that morning, "This statue is almost certainly Aphrodite, there was a big cult following of her on the island. A gold statue of this type was probably part of the treasury of the Kings of Cyprus. It's not solid gold and melted down it might be worth a few thousand."

"Yes, but as an artefact it is worth much more. Even if you could put a price on it," interrupted Joeanna.

"Yes, but difficult to sell," I said, "I don't think you will have buyers queuing at your door," I still could see no real future in the enterprise.

"I have a buyer," said Bull quietly.

These four words achieved the effect he was obviously looking for, silence. But he kept us waiting while he took a sip of coffee. I had to admit to a sneaking admiration for Bull, it was clear he had rehearsed the whole thing.

"I have a buyer, who will give us half a million pounds for the statue in cash when delivered to him. He has seen all this and believes she came from the Sanctuary of Aphrodite on the south coast of the island. What we have to do is fund the enterprise until delivery."

"How much are we talking about?" asked Joeanna.

"We should be able to do it for about ten thousand."

Bull picked up his coffee cup as the room went silent. I could feel his eyes on me over the rim of his cup. But he was looking at the wrong person, I think on that day I had about one hundred and fifty pounds in the bank and an overdraft for the business in four figures. I guessed he did not have much either which was why he was sat in our house. Joeanna had made no comment when the ten thousand was mentioned, which meant she could raise it.

Those eyes got on my nerves; I got up and walked to the window. Rain was lashing down outside. The garden looked battered and drenched in the light from the lounge. The thought of Cyprus was tempting, but ten thousand was a small fortune, and what would I find there, should you ever try to go back? And could we trust Bull?

"Would you use a small boat to get it out?" I asked still looking out of the window.

"That's right, we charter a small boat from another island, sail over and pick up the lady. Just like a Med cruise."

"Sounds wonderful," said Joeanna.

Closing the curtains I turned back to the room, one thing I knew for certain it was not going to be easy. Bull was smoking a thin rolled cigarette. I shared my thoughts with them.

"One thing, this is not going to be easy. The Cypriots will not take kindly to looters and smugglers, which, my dear, is what we will be," Joeanna glared at me but remained silent, "Why not hire the boat in Cyprus?" I continued, taking my seat again.

"Less suspicious. This way no local owner will be asking a lot of questions."

Bull was right again, it might be more expensive but much safer sailing away from one island on a cruise rather than hanging about Cyprus.

"Let's have a look at those maps," I said, my arguments for the moment exhausted.

For the next three hours we poured over maps of Cyprus, even Jan Wenmouth's map of the Troodos Mountains, on which the long dead man had marked the spot where the lady lay. It all felt a bit morbid to me but did not seem to affect Bull at all. Joeanna soon got bored and went to the kitchen to attend to the dinner dishes, after which she brought more coffee and we finished off the brandy.

By the time Bull left, it was near one a.m., his plan was pretty clear. I said we would sleep on it but knew already, Joeanna had swallowed the whole thing and we would be going. He would not accept a lift back to his hotel, although neither of us was in a fit state to drive him, or the offer of the spare room.

His plan was simple. We would fly out to Rhodes or Crete, hire a boat or perhaps even buy one; apparently he was a good sailor, something he had picked up over the years. Although a former marine, I had done no sea time, and had not been a weekend sailor either, but I could learn and was already aiming for the library and books on sailing. From whichever island we chose we would sail to Cyprus, to the north western corner. Hire some local transport, dig up the lady, and bring her down at night to a small cove.

Return the transport, so as not to draw attention to ourselves then sail north. The buyer would be waiting on the Turkish coast only forty odd miles away, it certainly appeared straight forward almost foolproof. But there were things nagging me, all the arrangements were through Bull. And another thing, how did he have Jan's map, the map of a dead man?

He wanted another crew member. Again he had someone lined up good with small boats who knew the eastern Mediterranean well. It seemed to me the only reason he needed us was money, and it was probably easier to sell it to us as I had been there rather than any stranger. But one thing was for sure he was not doing this out of the goodness of his heart.

Five

It gnawed at me, we knew nothing about Bull Moore. What had he been up to for the last eighteen years? How had he managed to locate me after all this time? And why the rush now? The statue had been there a long time; a few more weeks should make no difference. I raised these points with Joeanna as we lay in bed, we had separate beds but shared the same room I think she thought it frustrated me but quite frankly I was indifferent by that stage in our marriage.

"Look Mike, it will be fun, a bit of an adventure. Ye Gods, don't you think we need something in our lives?" She sat up in bed, "Just make a list and ask Bull tomorrow, and I'm sure you will get plain simple answers. And then all we have to say is yes."

I switched on the light and got up, "I'm going down to look at the maps again."

"Do what you like," she said burrowing deep into the bedclothes, "I'm going to dream of treasure and getting bloody rich."

It was gone four before I fell asleep on the settee. Another session with the maps and reading about Cyprus in the encyclopaedia had got me no further forward. One thing was certain; I was just as keen as Joeanna to get bloody rich as she put it and to escape my circumstances at that time. It was just this nagging, as if some kind of furies were there in the background.

Then there was Ginger Taff, was that a coincidence it surely must be. About a year before, I had met Ginger Taff the only other survivor of two section again. It had been the result of a bust up with Joeanna one of our many

40

rows. This one was a bit out of the ordinary in that I stormed off on my own for a few days.

With the Morris Van I headed down to Cornwall. Crossing the Tamar Bridge from Devon into Cornwall at Saltash, I stopped at the Rodney Inn, a modern sort of pub with a big car park. Why there at that pub I don't know, other than I wanted a rest and a drink before starting to hunt for somewhere to stay. And who should I find behind the bar but Ginger Taff. He did not recognise me at first, or he might have had that thing we all get from time to time he did not want to resurrect the past, but in his case I now know for certain it was the former.

When I spoke, his face lit up and he said, "Blow me down, Mike Harris, what's doing, boy'oh? The last time I saw you you'd been blown to bits on Cyprus."

"Yes, and the last time I saw you, you ginger haired Welshman you were running around like a headless chicken."

That weekend I stayed at the Rodney with Ginger Taff who was not only the landlord but the owner too. We went out fishing, drank quite a bit, and went over old times.

Ginger Taff had stayed in the Corps for twelve years after the Cyprus deployment, but he did not take part in Operation Musketeer, the Suez landings. On the way from Cyprus back to Malta, prior to the landings in Egypt, he'd fallen on board ship and broken a leg and spent several weeks in a hospital on Malta. So he could not tell me in detail what took place other than the section got shot up and Bull Moore was the only survivor. Although some of the other company members felt Bull was too trigger happy and glad he was not their bren gunner. Ginger did not meet Bull again who seemed to disappear after he'd served his time.

We did talk a little about the statue but just to wonder if it was still there. Which we had to admit, due to its remote location, the odds were it still was. Half heartedly we did talk about going back to Cyprus. But it was obvious Ginger Taff had done well for himself, he ran a nearly new Jaguar E Type coupé and perhaps he got the impression I was doing well.

Over the weeks and months we saw a lot of each other. We went walking quite a bit up on Dartmoor exploring our old Commando training haunts, or along the Cornish coastal paths and fishing as well. Perhaps Joeanna thought I had another woman but if she did, she did not seem to care or take any interest.

Then the news came he'd slipped on a coastal path, fallen down a cliff and died in the fall of massive head injuries. It cut me up quite badly, I found it hard to believe, you see I knew the path well; to fall there seemed absurd after all that had happened. All we had been through.

I was even more dumbstruck when Ginger Taff left his E Type Jaguar to me. His pride and joy, a British Racing Green fixed head coupé with wire wheels a 4.2 litre six cylinder engine. The funny thing was Ginger Taff was not all that tall and I doubted he could see the end of that lovely curved bonnet. Mind you he never drove it that fast anyway. And more often than not when we got together he would throw me the keys.

"You drive Mike, give her some stick, blow the cobwebs out," he would laugh. Then he would be holding onto the seat like a white knuckle ride if we went much over eighty. Perhaps it gave him a thrill, who knows he was a bit of a strange cove in some ways, but my oppo all the same. He must have only changed his will days before the accident. Later, I found out from his solicitor he had not changed his will rather it was the first one he had made. Had he had some sort of predestination of the future?

The funeral service was at St. Steven's Church in Saltash. There was a mizzling rain all that day to add to the sombre air. Perhaps a dozen people were there none of which I knew. Although somebody must have been in touch with the Corps, probably through the British Legion because a Marine Bugler in blues dress uniform turned up to play 'The Last Post'. The dozen mourners croaked their way through "Guide me O Thou great Jehovah" by William Williams 1717-91. The vicar did his best to aid us with some gusto but it was a pretty poor effort. I imagined Ginger Taff in the coffin groaning, "that's pathetic," and William Williams hurling brimstone and fire upon us from his heavenly perch.

And then Ginger Taff went on his last journey to the crematorium. I did not go there and felt a bit guilty about that later when he left me the Jag. Here was a friend I had found and lost again in a few months.

Now, twelve months later, and the only other survivor of two section had turned up on my doorstep. Was it coincidence? It did not feel like one but there was nothing to prove otherwise. So I just locked it away in the back of my mind.

*

Later that night, my mind did return to a windswept railway station beside the Exe estuary in Devon in February 1955.

A large Royal Marine Corporal had been waiting for us at the station, he was softly spoken, as if he actually felt sorry for us, he took our joining papers. There must have been fifty of us on that platform, National Servicemen. One or two with Teddy Boy haircuts. But everybody in the peak of condition, no flat feet or fallen arches here, we had all been passed at the medical several weeks earlier Grade One, all between eighteen and twenty-one. We were in for two years at Her Majesty's pleasure starting with sixteen weeks training.

When the Corporal had collected all the papers, he ushered us outside where we clambered into two four-tonne trucks with canopies, and started the short journey to the Commando training centre. The atmosphere was thick with apprehension in those trucks. A few people introduced themselves to the person sat beside them but most remained silent with their own thoughts and not a little apprehension. I remember thinking what the hell had I let myself in for.

The camp was a few miles up-stream from Exmouth but still on the banks of the river. It consisted of rows of uninviting wooden nissen huts and some new barrack blocks and canteens. We were dropped outside some huts, detailed off in a dozen to a hut and told to pick a bed space and make ourselves at home.

The hut was hardly cosy, it contained six iron bunks in pairs opposite each other with a straw filled mattress and no bedding, at the head of each bunk was a locker. In the centre of the hut was an ancient coal-burning stove which looked hardly adequate to warm the hut. Everything looked as if it was left over from the last war or even the one before that. I suppose I had not expected the Ritz but had hoped for a few more home comforts. But Hut 9 was home for the next sixteen weeks.

"Right yous lot, out here at the double," came a booming Scottish voice from our front door, interrupting our dazed awe at our accommodation.

So we all piled out of the huts, forty-eight of us had taken over four of them, 9-12. Outside stood a ramrod straight sergeant, I had never seen anyone quite so immaculate or upright.

"Fall in three ranks," he barked out, "You're not civvies now, get a move on. That's right three nice rows of twelve. Oh men, canny you count?"

After we had been scuffling around for a few seconds, that voice erupted again grabbing our attention, "Stand still. Right you shower," at more of a normal level of volume, "I take it you all understand the Queens English. No Welsh or Cornish speakers, I would advise not to try that one. You lot are now 415 squad. And you're Bravo Company, remember those two things and when I come along to you and give you your service number remember that too, always. Give me your name and religion when I come up to you. This is so we know how to bury you when we blow you up or you's end up shooting each other.

There are only two religions, Church of England or Roman Catholic that's C of E or R.C., no church of Turkey or anything else so you have a choice of two. My name is Sergeant Patterson that's P.A.T.T.E.R.S.O.N. Patterson, remember it. I am for my sins your troop sergeant. Your mum and dad all rolled into one for the next sixteen weeks. I'm like your service number you'll never forget me as long as you live."

Out of the six of us who were on that patrol in Cyprus, Patterson arrived at lanky spotty Stevens first.

"Name."

"Jeremy Falconer Stevens, Sergeant Corpse, Church of England, I think."

"Did your parents no love you Jeremy Falconer? And I'm no a corpse I'm a sergeant. I wear three stripes some thing you's lot are never likely to do. As I've got one more I'm higher up the tree than a corporal who has two. And just remember it's sergeants that run the Royal Marines and there are no sergeant-corporals in this here corps. There may be in other organisations, the yanks may have them or the RAF crap but not here my brave lads."

"Christ, I wish I'd joined the RAF," someone murmured along the line.

Sergeant Patterson allowed the trace of a smile to cross his face and let the comment pass on that occasion. This Sergeant had been everywhere from the beaches of D-Day to the bitter cold of Korea, and he had seen everything.

"Well, Jeremy Falconer, did ye no understand the question?"

"Could you repeat it, sergeant?"

Forget it, your number, Jeremy Falconer Stevens, is 411915, got it?"

"Yes, sergeant."

"Owen Lloyd, sergeant," was the next of the six, "chapel, I think," he said with a stupid grin on his face.

"Ye Gods, a ginger haired taffy. Now it might have missed you, pal, but chapel was no on our list of two. C of E or RC was the choice."

"Oh, I suppose it would have to be C of E. Seems a bit unfair, sergeant, if you know what I mean."

"There's nothing fair about the Royal Marines," said Patterson in a consolatory tone, "perhaps you should have enrolled in the Jehovah's Witnesses." Patterson took one step back to address the whole squad.

"In the Royal Marines we do everything the Pussers way. Your boots are pusser's boots, your religious advisors are pusser's Chaplins, but we are not totally heartless we give you a choice C of E or RC, got it, that's the pusser's choice. And we don't have any atheists or non-bloody-conformists," he took a step forward closer to Lloyd, "so what's it to be, Ginger Taff, not that I'm trying to rush you," he said in a soft friendly voice.

"Well, C of E if you put it like that, sergeant, thank you."

Patterson came to Bull Moore next.

"Paul Hugh Moore, C of E, sergeant."

The sergeant's eyes narrowed as he took in Bull. But he merely said, "Ah, Moore, have to keep an eye on you."

I was next out of the six. My number was 411922 and I was C of E, and yes it's true you never forget that number, you're more likely to forget your date of birth than your service number.

"Jack Kirkpatrick, sergeant, from Glasgow, Church of England and proud of it."

"Scraping the barrel here, a Scottish Orange-Man," said Patterson shaking his head in disgust, although he himself had come from Glasgow we later learnt.

Yorky Wright was the last one who was in that ill-fated section, "Reginald John Compton Wright, sergeant, RC," and his number was 411931.

At six a.m. the next morning, the notes of reveille blared out in our ice-box of a hut through the tannoy system. Moments after that the door was banged open with a crash as the duty Corporal Warner stamped into the hut.

"Hands off cocks, on with socks. Come on, wakey, wakey, get moving, are you stuck to those pits, perhaps I will have to help you. Come on half the day's gone rise and shine."

By the time he got to the end of the barrack hut and began his return anybody still not up was dragged out by the mattress.

"Out of those festering pits, come on lets get moving. Everything at the double now," that was his passing remark as he left for the next hut.

That day we visited various stores and collected various articles of clothing and equipment. We visited the MO, and his jolly sick bay attendants, we had several needles jabbed into various parts of the body, our balls felt and our various orifices examined. Then onto the dentist for an examination, and we had our hair cut.

"Everything under the beret," explained Patterson, "is yours, everything outside is mine and no different styles other than that."

"A pusser's style, sergeant," we all shouted.

"Well done men, you're learning."

We met our company commander a Captain Lake, who looked like he was left over from World War two where something nasty had happened to him. He informed us we were a cut above other National Servicemen. As although we had been conscripted, like everybody else, we had chosen to serve in the Royal Marines which in a manner of speaking was true.

"You could just have been idle slackers in the Pioneer Corps, and spent your two years at Aldershot pulling your plonkers. Having joined this illustrious corps you will see something of the world. And perhaps who knows if you are lucky some action."

The thought of seeing something of the world quite appealed to me, but I was not so sure about the action. He informed us we would be confined to the camp for the first six weeks and paid on Thursday.

"Excuse me, Captain, Sir," asked Ginger Taff, "how much do we get paid a week if you know what I mean?"

"Ye Gods," barked Patterson, "all officers are sir; you don't put their rank in front of that. Thirty bob I think is your scale of pay."

"Thirty bob," muttered Stevens, "that's only pocket money."

"Thank you, sergeant," said Lake who then continued to drone on about the history of the Corps we had deemed to join, by the end most of us found it hard to stay awake.

Six

The next day was our first proper parade, at 06.30 in denims, boots, and beret. No belts or anklets. Patterson inspected the parade.

"Did you shave this morning?"

"Yes, sergeant."

"Well, stand closer to the razor next time."

We looked truly like Fred Karno's Army.

"Did you sleep in those denims? That beret looks like the flight deck of the Ark Royal. What are those horrible spots on your face?"

"Acne, sergeant."

"Acne? Looks more like leprosy, report to the MO after parade lad. Royal Marines do not get bloody acne."

We met our section corporal then, who would be with us through thick and thin, Corporal Dennis Double, a likeable cockney, and a three badger, three good conduct badges one for every three years, who had been in the Corps ten years. If Patterson was our mother and father, Double was like an older brother.

From then on we seemed to run everywhere. Run to the lectures, and back from the lectures. Run to the assault course, and run around it. Run to the start of the run and run around the run. Run to the parade ground then march around the parade ground. And if not running we were polishing things, cleaning things, scrubbing things, we were never allowed to be idle. Don't stop for a minute keep them going from dawn to dusk.

And so the weeks went by. Shooting on the range, bayonet charging, unarmed combat. Drill and drill and more drill. Lectures. Swimming test. First aid. More drill.

Eating and sleeping everything went by in a blur. Until Saturdays when there was no parade or anything. Even Sundays you had church parade. Nothing to clean, nothing to do and nowhere to go other than the NAAFI canteen, the NAAFI, no-ambition-and -fug-all-interest. All they had there was some sticky buns, weak beer and a couple of women older than most bloke's grannies.

*

Over the weeks, the change, the metamorphosis in us was startling. We were no longer factory drones, city gents, or mechanics. We were tough, hardened, we no longer got out of breath at the slightest exertion. Now we could run miles and hold a conversation at the end, or more important fight a battle, with a verity of weapons we had been trained on.

We learnt cunning, some were better at it than others. How to get out of duties and fatigues never to volunteer for anything you got volunteered enough as it was. It was no good complaining, do not get caught was the motto, undetected crime is no crime. Your only duty was to your oppo, your pal watching your back, not to the Queen or the Corps of Marines. Even if the Corps was founded in 1664 by Charles the Second the bloody merry monarch, known then as the Duke of York's and Albany's Maritime Regiment of foot, even it had captured the Rock of Gibraltar in 1704 and that was the only battle honour they wore because they had so many.

These were abstract things. Your duty was to your pal, your mates, but there were some. Loners, individuals, people who did not quite fit, Bull Moore was one of these. However Bull was good at everything to do with soldiering, he was a crack shot with an array of weapons. He was always within the first two or three on anything physical. Perhaps only map reading was his weakness. You wanted him on your side but at the same time you did not. It was that first run ashore that convinced me and most of our squad that Bull Moore was a sadist.

We were ready for this, all spick and span in our khaki Battle Dress with knife like creases, to show ourselves off to the local populace of Devon, the Janners. Our first run-ashore. Some chose Exmouth, we opted for the bright lights of Exeter it was bigger. I think it was seven or eight of us that went ashore that day together. Six of us who would be on the patrol in Cyprus and a couple of other faces that stare back at me from the squad photo but I don't remember their names now, the reason why you should always write things down. Bull Moore had been lying stretched out on his pit all booted and cleaned ready, but just staring vacantly at the wall when we were ready to go. He had already gained the sobriquet 'Bull', the raging Bull, like the Spanish Fighting Bulls. Mostly from the way he was able to almost smash his way around the assault course while others floundered.

"Come on, Bull," said Ginger Taff, "you're not going to lie on your pit when we can go ashore. Think of all those gals waiting for the likes of us. Panting for it boy'oh."

"Well," said Bull, slowly, menacingly getting to his feet, a thin smile on his face, "if you put it like that and seeing you fellers are inviting me I think I'll tag along."

It was less than an hour later we were tumbling from the bus in Exeter Bus Station. We were soon in the heady atmosphere, smoke and ale, of a pub on a Saturday lunch time. It was full of Marines, and girls, Stevens thought most of them looked, 'jolly nice' while Ginger Taff thought they were, 'scrubbers'.

Bull Moore seemed to have no opinion about the fairer sex. We drank steadily for an hour or more. The activities at camp were the prime topic of our conversation. It was Kirkpatrick who started the ruckus at the bar with two sailors, he was noisy and slurring his words after six pints in such a short space of time and a prime candidate for trouble.

"Bleedin' matelots, never any good when it comes to fighting mate; it's us that have to do it."

The short fat three-badged stoker grinned, "Oh yeah, and just how many actions have you been in, you thick paddy. The battle of the prams." Which brought hoots of laughter from many corners of the bar, "Surprising the Corps take people like you, too thick for the Navy. You ain't even got one of them green hats yet sonny."

"I'm a thick Paddy, Jock," said Kirkpatrick going red in the face. By this time Stevens had a restraining hand on Kirkpatrick.

"Well Jock-Orange," said Stevens, "I think we had better leave these old sea dogs to it."

"No, I think we are owed an apology," said the other matelot, rising from where he had been leaning against the bar, where the first sailor was short and fat this one was tall and broad. Kirkpatrick gulped.

"I think you're absolutely right, old boy," said Stevens, "come on Jock-Orange, apologise to these nice boys in blue."

Jock-Orange muttered something barely audible.

"Bleedin' Paddys," said the fat sailor as Stevens steered Jock-Orange away from the bar.

Fury creased his face and he shrugged off Stevens's loose grip, swivelled and kicked the second matelot in the shin with his steel tipped boot.

This had a rippling effect throughout the bar. The tall matelot slumped against the bar reaching down to his bruised shin scattering drinks along the bar counter. A civvy nearby, seeing his pint sailing off the bar, took a swing at him but hit a marine passing by with two pints in his hands. Within seconds the bar resembled a big fight from some western saloon. We were all out through a side door dragging Jock-Orange with us. Stevens and I jammed the door handles with a broom handle.

"That should hold them for a few minutes," I said.

"Ha, where's Bull?" shouted Ginger Taff.

We all rushed around to the front of the pub to see if he was there. As we arrived, the fat stoker came out through the window head first. Bull came flying out after him. The stoker crumpled into the ground and did not move.

Bull landed on all fours cat like and sprang to his feet under control in one move. And then was on the stoker kicking him savagely in the body and head. It took all of us to drag him away and keep Jock-Orange from joining in beating the stoker.

"Jesus Christ," said Yorky Wright, "you'll kill the guy that way."

"He deserved a good slapping," said Bull regaining his composure, "you lot should have never dragged me off. Don't interfere again if you know what's good for you."

He was nearly calm now but the frenzy had been frightening to witness.

"Stand by your beds," said Sergeant Patterson, an evening two days later on entering hut 9.

He marched seemingly for once unsure of himself into the middle of the hut and warmed his hands at the stove. Corporal Double stood by the door with the nearest thing to a scowl he could manage on his face.

"Yous lot listen and listen good. A little bird has told me a story about a fight in a pub in Exeter between matelots and marines. Not an unusual occurence I ken you're going to say, there has always been friendly rivalry between us which sometimes gets out of hand," he smiled and nodded, "even been in one or two disputes myself. But one of the matelots from this Exeter fight ended up in hospital and will be invalided out the service. Brain damage they say, got a wife and kids too," he stopped talking and walked to the end of the hut, as if he were merely on an inspection tour. There he turned and stopped, 'If I thought anybody in here, or in any other of the huts under my charge, had anything to do with it I would move heaven and earth to get the bastard locked up," he moved back to the centre of the hut and stopped directly in front of Bull, "nothing to do with you Moore?" He said between clenched teeth.

"No, sergeant," said Bull without flinching, leaving a hurt expression on his face.

"I got my eye on you laddy, just remember that. Carry on men," and Patterson left the hut.

Bull Moore did not go ashore again while we were in Devon, he always found himself on duty or fatigues, but he never complained about Patterson's obvious victimisation and neither did anybody else. But it was only a few weeks later and we had our green berets and left for the hotspots of the Mediterranean.

*

It had been much the same when we got to Malta, one of the last bastions of the British Empire. Runs ashore were fraught with danger. The trouble being Bull Moore usually tagged along. Most people were just too plain scared of him to turn him down.

That golden brown collection of rocks like three stepping stones between Europe and Africa had too many exotic temptations for young men with high levels of testosterone. Young men who had never left Albion's misty shores, we should have been given some guidance, not bromide in the tea, and a lecture by a spotty young Naval Doctor on the perils of sexual diseases.

Valletta was our undoing amid that town's narrow streets. From a distance its towering battlements, a high-point of the art of medieval military architecture even fairy-tale mythical in their structure, were alluring. But get below those lofty ramparts, underneath, grovelling enclosed by those majestic walls where the sun never reached, lived a low life in the bars and brothels, the high-light of many a run-ashore.

Strait Street in Valletta, a medieval cobbled alley hump like at the start then running steeply to the waterfront, the Navy infamously named it the Gut. It was a favourite for a yarn on mess decks and in barrack blocks all over the Empire. By the time we got there the sun was beginning to well and truly set on it. It was here in this underworld, strangely enough, that Bull Moore fell in love, if love is quite the right term. Given it was an all consuming obsessive emotion that was eating him up.

54

Bull fell in love with a whore of mixed parentage. Exotic some might say, she was the daughter of a White Russian mother who had fled her home-land sometime in the nineteen twenties during that country's interminable civil wars and purges. She came from an aristocratic family, her father a Count shot by the Bolsheviks along with almost all the other members of the family at some time. Quite how she arrived in Malta was not known, not even her real name, for she took the name Morris apparently after the first sailor she took to her bed. But she did name her daughter after the last Tsar's daughter Anastasia. The daughter did not know her father, other than he must have been white. Anastasia at times insisted he was a British Admiral, but this only to give herself a more colourful parentage.

Anastasia was, even at her age, stunning, regal in her bearing, if somewhat seedy in her dress. Some of her clothes appeared like those her mother might have worn at the Palace of the Tsar but this was all part of an act. By the time Bull Moore came on the scene, Anastasia was well past thirty and looking for a ticket out of that life.

It was a surprise to us shortly after our arrival, and by us I mean Ginger Taff, Yorky, Jock Orange, Lanky spotty Stevens, and I, that Bull told us he had a girl. For he had shown little interest in females back home in the few months we had known him. His situation became a joke behind his back when her profession was discovered but never to his face. Bull's infatuation became a dangerous slide. This coincided with us becoming Corporal Jan Wenmouth's "sprongs" in his "nursery school."

"I'm Jan Wenmouth," he announced the first morning he met us, in his slow West Country drawl, "and we are going to be two section. We cannot call ourselves a section yet. Why? Because you are wet behind the ears. Now, the first thing to learn sharpish is to forget Lympstone, here you start learning for real. Here, what you learn, if you're lucky, might just keep you alive."

Jan had been in the Marines since World War Two, he had seen action with the Partisans in Yugoslavia, what

55

he did not know about soldiering was not worth knowing. He was in for twenty-two years longer if he could manage it. They would have to throw him out before he would leave voluntarily and then he might chain himself to the railings outside Stonehouse Barracks Plymouth. He was tall and thin with a hooked nose. On a ten mile speed march, in full fighting order, he would barely break into a sweat. He always looked immaculate even if he had been out chasing terrorists for a week. But he taught us to trust no one, other than your oppo who watched your back, and to trust nothing, unless it was Pussers issue, and not to put too much faith in that either.

Jan did not frequent the Gut nor had any apparent need for its services. He had a wife and two kid's home in Honiton. He was essentially a private man and did not confide in us. He may have been waiting until we came up to his standards. Given this, it was strange he agreed to bury the statue in the first place and gave voice to returning. Perhaps he saw it as a boost to his pension. Or maybe better to let sleeping dogs lie and we would never return anyway to collect it. But it was Jan who had marked the map so clearly.

Jan soon had Bull marked as a sloppy bully, who turned to on parade like a recruit in Fred Karno's Army. At first he took him aside trying the fatherly approach which made Bull defensive.

"What's the matter with Bull?" he asked us one fine morning after parade. Bull had been duty the night before and was not there. Nobody answered.

"Don't all speak at once? Look's like he's on drugs, at this rate he's heading for the cells."

"That would be easy," piped up Ginger Taff.

"He's got a woman," I said.

"Nothing wrong with that," shrugged Jan, "not a whore surely?" it suddenly dawned on him.

"And she's taking him for every penny he's got and some he hasn't," said Spotty Stevens.

"Borrowing money?"

We nodded in unison.

56

"Well that's great."

"He's sort of hard to say no to," I said.

"What a bunch of heroes. So you help your section mate get deeper in the shit."

Within hours, Jan had arranged for the brothel to be raided by the MPs among who he had several friends. They found Bull there, a punch-up began and Bull got fourteen days confined to camp and extra duties.

We all hoped cold-turkey might cure the disease. But it was a double edged sword, for absence in this case made the heart grow fonder. And Bull had not been fined. For amid the carnage of the punch-up Bull had come quietly, which was a surprise but showed the level of his infatuation. The two weeks gave Bull the chance to repair his battered finances. Even with his extra duties he managed too fit in some more duties he did for others at the going rate of five bob for mess duties, and a ten bob note for twenty four hour guard.

None of us knew whether it had worked, for Bull did not mention Anastasia. That was until the day before his fourteen days were up. And he told Spotty Stevens he was going to desert go AWOL and take Anastasia with him. Asking his advice, being the most educated which countries to head for. This time we told Jan. Who tried a different approach going to the brothel and telling Anastasia what Bull intended for her. It was certainly unwelcome news to her and she quickly disappeared into the interior of the island. The "buzz" was she went into a convent rather than have a life with Bull she had not bargained for.

It did not end there, for Bull took the place apart looking for her. This time he was heading for the glass-house. That was until the whole Brigade got orders to move to Cyprus.

It was then Bull took to wearing a silver cross. A Russian Orthodox cross with the two bars, we guessed Anastasia had given it to him. Real Russian silver by all accounts on a strong chain, Bull never mentioned her again and neither did any of us to him.

Bull was still wearing that cross when he turned up eighteen years later. Did he know what had happened, had he found out before the Suez operation. Had he taken bloody revenge on those who had interfered in his life, with the best of intentions, in the dusty streets and wharf houses of Port Said? It was something I could not believe.

Would it be safe to bring up the subject after all these years? Was it even worth the trouble? Bull was, or had been, a psychotic, some thing like this might lie just below the surface or was he now just as sane as anyone. But who was I to judge? Was it normal for someone of my age, on the whole an honest citizen, to set out on a career of crime? For lifting that statue would be a criminal act, something that could get us several years in a Cypriot prison. Though Joeanna and Bull appeared not even to have considered it.

Seven

Joeanna was up by eight the next day and as always in the mornings irritatingly cheerful, while I was slow and usually bad tempered. I had a headache as well after all that dreaming and trying to remember things that happened twenty years before. She did not mention the night before which caught me off balance for I expected an argument. She was quickly gone, to an antique sale, something else she dabbled in. It was an embarrassing fact, at that time her hobby netted more cash than my business. But then Joeanna always had the ability to make money, sometimes I thought she was on the game but somehow I knew better, perhaps I just wanted to think she was.

I had known deep down soon after Bull walked through my garage doors that I would return to Cyprus. But what I had not bargained for was Joeanna coming along, still it could not be helped and it would perhaps hasten the time we went our separate ways.

After nine I phoned Bull's hotel and told him to count us in. He did not seem surprised, or come to that pleased, but agreed to meet again in a couple of days when he would bring along the fourth member to introduce him by which time we should have the money ready.

My day was spent closing up the garage. I put a dust sheet over the E Type after running it around the block.

The rest of the day I spent in the town library studying books on seamanship and basic navigation and taking notes. After three hours on that, some time on Aphrodite and the Greek Myths was a welcome relief.

At five, the Librarian had to ask me to leave as they were waiting to lock up.

"You could always join the library," she suggested.

I nodded agreement but hurried away there was no time for that. I could have pinched the books but had not thought of that, after all I was off to pinch a priceless artefact.

Joeanna was at home when I got back. The fact I had agreed to the enterprise was tantamount to a ceasefire in our relationship, which I suppose was a relief for both of us. That night, a phone call from Bull told me to book four tickets to Crete on the next available flight.

Events went forward rapidly the next day. Joeanna booked four return tickets to Crete leaving in five days time and a villa on the south coast of the island at Matala plus a hire car waiting at Iraklion Airport, while I changed several thousand pounds into travellers' cheques in British pounds and US dollars, which we split between us. That had been Joeanna's idea to make Bull a little more reliant on us as we held the purse strings.

We did not see Bull again or meet Donald Temple for the first time until we met at the Olympic Airways check in desk Gatwick Airport. Bull's excuse seemed weak to me in that he had to return up north on some family business.

Donald Temple was a tall muscular young man with a mop of straw coloured hair in his late twenties with a South African accent. He was dressed in jeans with a matching jacket with just a large holdall for baggage.

Bull had undergone something of a transformation his seedy look had gone. He was now dressed in an expensive beige lightweight suit, and black stitched leather shoes, his luggage consisted of an expensive leather briefcase and a rather battered holdall. He looked very much the seasoned traveller.

We kept to two separate groups waiting for our departure, which felt like taking security to extremes. After all we were not criminals. But then it struck me that Bull and the mysterious Mr. Temple might have police records.

Joeanna was sick shortly after take off. Fellow passengers were glad to hear from me it was only nerves

60

and she did not really like flying. I just hoped none had seen her consume several large whiskeys before the flight. An hour later she was asleep. I found sleep impossible in the cramped conditions that made my left foot ache even after all those years. Still I read the in-flight magazine which had an article on Crete and walking in the mountains I made a mental note about carrying enough water and salt.

My mind began to wander toward that other island to the east and for the first time I felt not only was our little group wasting its time but I was more than the others dreaming about the past. To hope to find a statue buried in a pine plantation for eighteen years the odds must be long. Pines grew rapidly, they would cut them down, get rid of the roots. How did they do that, dig them up or burn them out? Surely our gold lady would have been found by now. But no, Bull would have checked on that such a discovery I guessed would not have gone unnoticed. Unless they sold it on the black market too, that thought struck me as funny.

And then there was Eleni, she might be dead, or moved from Cyprus, and if not, did I have the right to come back, to go blundering about in her life just because my own was not blissfully happy? I tried not to think too much about her.

"This is your Captain speaking, we will shortly be arriving at Iraklion, thank you for flying," thus my thoughts were interrupted. There was no going back now; we would have to see the enterprise through to the end.

Part Two

July 15, 1974

The Greek Colonels hatch their plot to topple Arch Bishop Makarios, President of Cyprus, and replace him with a pro-Enosis (Union with Greece) president which will mean de facto Union with Greece.

BBC News.

"In Cyprus, President Makarios has been overthrown. The National Guard broadcasting over Cyprus Radio claims that the President was killed during an early morning assault on the Presidential Palace in Nicosia. However, news of his death has not been confirmed."

On the night of July 19, a RAF Nimrod X-Ray Victor 241, from No 303 Squadron, in the maritime reconnaissance role, took off from Luqa Airbase Malta. It climbed into a starlit night sky turning east, its objective the island of Cyprus just over 1000 miles away.

X-Ray Victor 241 pilots were initially disappointed at missing the Annual Summer Ball in the Officers Mess that night, but were about to see history in the making. From 150 miles out, the crew could clearly see fires burning out of control on the Troodos Mountains, they were soon down to low level above the invasion fleet off Kyrenia. Although scanned by search and fire control radars no anti aircraft guns in the Turkish Fleet were pointed at the aircraft.

On that same July day, the Commando Carrier HMS Hermes with 41 Commando Royal Marines arrived off the southern shore of Cyprus. Hermes had arrived off

Malta, home for 41 Commando, three days earlier after a deployment to the USA and Canada. However, the declining situation on Cyprus had required the diversion to the island for an "indefinite period."

Two thousand three hundred airline miles to the north-west, the advance party of 40 Commando Royal Marines, the United Kingdom Land Forces spearhead Unit for July, had left Seaton Barracks Plymouth for RAF Lyneham and air transport to Cyprus to reinforce the garrison. Nobody knew for certain just what the Turkish invasion might mean.

Eight

Irakalion International Airport barely deserved that title, for it consisted of a few scruffy buildings and a pothole strewn runway. On which, during our landing, the pilot seemed to find most of them. Joeanna clutched my arm tightly, she was white with fear and I guess a bit of a hangover did not help. I suspect it was only the imminent promise of release from the aircraft that kept her from throwing up again.

Even though it was two hours before dawn, the heat and smell of the Mediterranean caressed my senses. In a few hours the temperature would be climbing toward a hundred degrees, my shirt was already sticky just walking to the airport buildings. All went smoothly getting into Crete, the officials met us with bored indifference. The hire car was ready just a few forms to sign, and baggage reclaim had been boring and painless.

By the time we had reached the open road, in the Fiat saloon, the sky to the east had a rim of light. The road from Iraklion to Matala runs virtually due south and climbs through some spectacular scenery of the White Mountains soon after leaving the north coast. Not that our cheerful band had much of the tourist inclination about them. Even so, we had to stop after an hour for Joeanna to be sick again, after which she curled up in the back seat and was soon asleep again, gently snoring. Donald dropped off to sleep as well his head resting against the window which looked uncomfortable.

"You better do something about your Mrs, Mike. This drinking is likely to draw to much attention to us."

"You must be joking, Bull. She's not one to take any notice of me. Anyway after this episode I would think she'll lay off the booze for a time. And it had more to do with flying than any thing else."

"She doesn't strike me as being scared of flying, hard to believe that. But all the same you better make sure. I don't want her blabbing her mouth off."

I just shrugged my shoulders in reply.

Bull's attitude got under my skin, what did it matter to him? We would only be here a few days at the most and then at sea. And it was Joeanna who had put the money up not that he knew that. But I let it go, enough trouble I felt lay ahead without starting a trial of strength now.

Bull reading the map had me take a wrong turning, so his map reading had not improved, with which we arrived in Mires a small town off the main road that would not have looked out of place in a western. There was a single seedy taverna in the town square, where we stopped, as we were all in need of some coffee to wake up. We sat at a wooden table on roughly hewn chairs. Joeanna looked pale and wore sun glasses against the glare of the morning sun.

"About an hour, probably less and we will be there," said Bull looking up from the map which he had spread on the table and he had discussed with the waiter in pigeon Greek. Donald stood yawning and generally trying to get his cramped limbs moving.

"One thing about this Matala," I observed, "it's off the beaten track, though it might make finding a boat more difficult."

"No sweat, man," said Donald, "know a feller; he's going to meet us at the villa tomorrow. Give us the run down on what he's got, right good feller used him before won't ask any fool questions man. You know the type."

"Sounds like you have done this before," said Joeanna.

"Yep, done thousands of miles in the Aegean and the Med, charter sailing, odd bit of smuggling even gun running you know. You got a fast boat you can make a buck or two."

The truth was we did not know, but I liked Donald's confident air. But how he and Bull could have got to know each other was a bit baffling.

We were soon on the road again. The temperature rapidly climbed, even the car blower on full cold gave little relief and I began to regret not getting a bigger model with full air conditioning.

Matala on the south coast is barely one hundred and fifty miles from the African shore, and our goal Cyprus, two hundred miles to the east. The village nestled around a small horseshoe bay. To the west, cliffs rose straight from the sea that were honeycombed with caves, natures work which over the years had been aided by man. The village had a few shops, tavernas small hotels, and a few villas for tourists although most stayed on the livelier north coast. A short elderly lady dressed in black, her face leathery brown from years under the sun, let us into our villa. This comprised yards of cool marble, simple wooden furniture and wooden shutters for the windows.

Joeanna raced away to the bathroom to repair the ravages of the long night, while we men unloaded the car. That done, I slipped into swimming trunks and made my way to the beach which although near the height of the season had few people on it.

The water was blood warm, and tiny fish darted around my feet as I waded out to deeper water. I stayed in the water about half an hour and then made my way to the village square.

It was at one of those shops you get in Greece rather like a haberdasher that sell everything, I heard the radio.

"The Presidential Palace in Nicosia has been attacked by Pro-Enosis troops; it would appear President Makarios is dead."

The shop keeper smiled at me as he hunched over the radio.

"You speak English?" I asked rather rudely.

"Yes, see speak very good English," he seemed not a bit put out by my manner.

"How old is the news from Cyprus?" I continued in a gentler more relaxed tone.

"Ah," his face lit up like all Greeks, I guessed he would love to speak politics, "just this morning. But very bad move, now the Turks must act. Our Government fools."

"You have radios for sale?"

"Oh yes, yes," he quickly returned with a small transistor radio and batteries.

"Still, no need to worry about Cyprus, have a nice holiday on Crete."

"Yes, but I have friends on Cyprus."

"Not so good for your friends, best they get out come to Crete," he finished grinning.

I paid hurriedly and left the shop. Back at the villa I found the place deserted, they must have all had similar ideas. Switching on the radio I tuned it to the BBC World Service and left it outside the bathroom while I had a quick shower to wash away the salt from the sea. Then, dressed in shorts and a shirt, my first instinct was to rush off and find the others. But I tried the door to the room Bull and Donald were in, it was not locked. Somehow I did not quite swallow honour among thieves, which in a few days we would be, a quick look at their gear and I might learn something useful.

Bull's gear was neat and tidy. Beside his bed was a book on sailing the Med and a couple of paperback thrillers. Most of his clothes on hangers in the wardrobe were fairly new, while in the bottom were an expensive but worn pair of walking boots, nothing that told me much about the man or his past.

Donald was not tidy like Bull but not untidy either. No reading material, but he had left his passport behind which told me he had been born in Dorset although now he was South African, as was the passport, he was twenty seven and a student or had been, the ten year passport only had two years left. He did not strike me like a student at all, but then what did I know about students. However, finding an automatic Browning pistol in the bottom of his holdall told me a lot and that Donald Temple was not what he seemed. Yet he could not be a professional either, bringing a pistol and enough ammunition to start a minor war through customs with all the hijacking of airliners that had been going on. What with all the terrorists about that was plain stupid, was he that stupid? But what if he had picked it up on Crete? Had he had chance since we arrived? The gun cast a long shadow over Donald in my mind if indeed that was his name.

Leaving the gun where I found it, I made my way to the taverna in the square where with any luck I expected to find the others. Bull called from a table there as I approached.

"What you drinking, Mike?"

"Something pretty stiff in view of the news," I said sitting beside Joeanna.

"Have a raki then, the local fire water, and what's the news?"

The magnitude of the events soon sank in and silence settled on our group, I was glad to see Joeanna on orange juice and with an empty plate in front of her.

"In the long run," said Bull, "this could work to our advantage. The Cyps will be distracted, even uninterested in ancient statues. Trying to kill each other that's their favourite sport." It was a good point.

"Yes, they might have their minds on other things and we might walk into a bloody war. People get hurt and killed in them you know," hissed Joeanna.

"I think Bull knows that, Joeanna, and you are jumping the gun a bit. We don't know what's happening. The news is very garbled nothing is certain."

"We should wait and see, get some more up to date information," added Donald.

He spoke fluent Greek which surprised me again and went off to try and find out what he could from the locals. But all he got was Union with Greece and reports

68

from Cyprus were garbled. We listened to my transistor radio for a while.

"There's something else on my mind," I turned to Donald, "why are you carrying a gun?" My question was met by silence, "I expect an answer or we can call the whole thing off."

Bull looked bewildered, his great head sank into his shoulders and a scowl crossed his face. So he knew nothing about the gun either.

"Not nice, searching a fellers clobber, man," said Donald with a grin on his face.

"Well, you know I'm not packing a gun," said Bull.

"Yes, but surely you and Donald come as a pair. You must know each other well."

"No," Bull was quick to a denial, "we met in a bar. I told him our problem getting to Cyprus by sea. He seemed to know a lot about the area and sailing so I hired him."

"Hired him," laughed Joeanna, "what with? It sounds more like he picked you up in a bar."

Donald was still grinning through this exchange.

"Donald, I think you better come clean about your background and why you are carrying the artillery."

"Yes, I would like to know that," said Bull but I waved him to silence.

Donald shrugged his shoulders, "Not much to tell. Studied ancient history at Jo'berg University, got a degree but no real work you could get your teeth into, other than some summer field trips out to the Peloponnese five years ago. But I had done quite a bit of sailing at home, man. So rather than go back, I got work crewing yachts out here. It's better to be poor in the sun you know. Did some petty smuggling until I had to leave Greece, it was getting hot. Was on my way home via London and met old Bull, he offered me a job, which was not entirely legal, thus the gun."

"Bit risky coming back to Greece?" I said.

"Not really, Mike, it was well over a year ago. Greece is in turmoil, what with the Colonels dictatorship," he lowered his voice here, "it would not surprise me if they fall from power over this Cyprus thing. The Yanks will see to that. And Crete's not the same as the mainland, and we won't be here long, or that's how I understand it." I nodded in reply.

"How much did he offer you?" asked Joeanna.

"Thousand pounds for the trip, bonus of five thousand if all goes well."

"You know what we are after?" I continued.

"Not exactly, just artefacts, but I guessed it's not legal."

I felt his answers were truthful as far as they went. But Bull had not been straight with us which I had half expected.

"I think you better tell us a bit about yourself, Bull."

"Bit late for twenty questions now when we are about to kick off."

"Oh, it's never too late," said Joeanna, malice in her voice.

I could tell Bull was getting angry; his eyes began to dart around the group of us.

"Just remember," continued Joeanna with the football theme, "the match could be postponed or even called off."

"Let's just keep it friendly," I interrupted, "nobody wants to call anything off. We are all in this together. Just tell us what you have been up too since 1956, Bull, I'm sure it's not top secret."

Donald sat forward his arms resting on the table as if not wanting to miss anything Bull had to say. A little strange I thought, but then Bull had strung him along as well.

"Well," began Bull, licking his lips composing himself, "after Suez, I left the mob. I went out to various wars, mainly in Africa as a soldier of fortune."

That was until they got too bloody and senseless even for him. An American friend got him a job in the States, where he had worked until just recently when US immigration had caught up with him and he had returned to the UK with the advice not to return to the US for quite some time. A lot of this was vague, but I could tell that was all we were going to get.

"That lady on Cyprus is my old age pension, that's all there, is to it. And it's about time we contact Donald's man about a boat. We are wasting time going over old history like this."

"OK," I said, "you better go off and do it."

"You trust those two?" said Joeanna when they had gone.

"Well not much, I must admit but we either do trust their greed or go home," and that was the bottom line and she had no answer to that.

Nine

That night, we all listened to the BBC World Service News which still carried the claim that Makarios was dead. Athens was being quiet about the whole affair, waiting for a reaction from Ankara. The Voice of America on CBS from Rhodes stated the situation was unclear and there was no confirmation on the death of Makarios or that civil war had broken out. All of which was no real help to us. But we reached a decision of sorts, to carry on as planned, have a look at a boat Donald had lined up while keeping an ear on the radio for events on Cyprus.

"Are you still awake?" said Joeanna.

The luminous dial on the travel alarm clock said 1.45. It must have been the excitement that kept us awake that night. We were in separate narrow hard beds.

"Yes, I'm awake," I knew what was on her mind for it was on mine as well, "it's no good worrying. The situation may work to our advantage, and if things get worse we call the whole thing off."

"What, with a gun at our heads? You should have got rid of that when you had the chance."

"Somehow, I don't think it's pointing at us," but I knew she was right.

"What do you mean it's not pointing at us?"

"I'm not sure, just a feeling I suppose."

"You're too trusting. I bet Bull's got a gun by now or he's getting one. They may even be in it together."

Now, that was one thing I did not suspect. I did respect Joeanna's female intuition but some how I could not see them working together and for what against us.

"There's something about those two I agree, but it's not working together. We could always insist Donald ditches the gun."

"Do you think he would agree?"

"Hard to say, we could always…"

I heard her breathing deepen, she was asleep. I was going to say we could always get some artillery ourselves, but no, that might only make matters worse. There was another trouble here on Crete, guns were easy to come by and really a ban would be impossible to enforce. Joeanna was right, Bull would get one if he did not have one already.

I awoke still feeling tired; it was already fully light outside. Joeanna was still asleep, unusual for her to sleep late, it was gone nine. Pulling on swimming trunks I made my way quietly outside, the villa was quiet with no sign of movement. The beach already had a number of sun worshippers on it and several people were in the sea swimming and on pedal boats.

However, what grabbed my attention, about one hundred and fifty yards from the beach, was a sleek white launch at anchor. Her lines looked ex-naval or like a fast rescue launch. One hundred and twenty foot in length with wide flared bows that told of great speed. Her superstructure seemed bare, not that I knew that much about boats, only an odd looking wheel house and aft a low hatch-way leading below. A short stubby mast protruded from the back of the wheel house with some shorter thin radio masts on the short spar of the main masts. Three figures came up from the aft hatch, but what really grabbed my attention, one was Bull.

My blood was boiling and perhaps it was a good job I had the delay of hiring a pedal boat and then making my way out to the launch. It soon became obvious it was Bull and Donald spending our money again. After all we had said yesterday, here they were going behind our backs. A third man was talking to them. He looked nothing like a sailor. Rather he belonged in an office, clean crisp white suit, and shoes to match, carrying a briefcase, his tanned face hidden by dark sunglasses.

All three took no notice of me and went below via the wheel house. But then, I did not call out. When I reached the launch I tied the pedal boat to one of the side rails where another dinghy was tied and clambered on board just as Bull's head came into view via the after hatch.

"Ah Mike," he said like a naughty little boy caught out and disappeared below again.

"What are you up to, Bull?" I called after him.

"We were about to wake you," he said re-emerging again from below, "felt you and Joeanna could do with a lay in, after such a long day yesterday. Need your beauty sleep."

"There is problem?" a voice from below called.

"No problem, just another member of our party. Come below, Mike, and meet Mr Kepal, he brought the boat around for our inspection."

"No, Mr Bull," Kepal greeted me with a wide grin, "this is not just a boat, this is the Argo."

I forced a smile and shook hands with Kepal who had the dark looks of the non Dorian Greeks, although his name appeared Turkish, but then they had ruled Crete for hundreds of years. Kepal dripped with gold watch, bracelets, rings, even teeth.

"Come on, Mike," said Donald like someone with a new toy, "I'll show you around the Argo, she's a real beauty, man."

He was in his element during our tour of inspection and he was thorough, I had to admit. The Argo had originally been a US Navy Patrol Boat brought to the Med toward the end of World War Two. She had never even seen action. Surplus to navy requirements after the war she had been sold off cheap rather than being taken back to America along with dozens of others.

"She's a bit long in the tooth then, Donald."

"Not really, as boats go," he said over his shoulder as he led me aft, "mind your head here," he continued as we arrived in the engine compartment which was surprisingly spacious, "she's been expertly converted after being let go a bit in the sixties."

The engine room took up about a third of her length, in which was mounted a powerful diesel engine. Fuel tanks comprised the sides and had been much larger at one time. Original power had come from two large high octane petrol aero engines that had provided power to the three propellers. Now there was only one. Donald explained all this as he clambered around the bilges and pipes like some demented monkey. Everything looked good on the engine, the engine oil was clean, as were the fuel filters and bowls and there were no leaks.

"What sort of range and speed has she got, Donald?"

My question was answered by more of the Argo's history. Her aero engines in the navy had consumed aviation fuel at the rate of something like two miles to the gallon, giving her a top speed around forty knots or forty-five miles an hour. However, the new engine took up far less room and the fuel tanks had been cut down to extend the accommodation. Even so, she could still manage about twenty knots, and at ten knots she had a range of some eight hundred miles on the two forty gallon tanks.

"With our trip, we might be able to make it without refuelling, or perhaps just a top up somewhere. Then again we could carry say half a dozen extra jerry cans that should see us through. Man, am I looking forward to this trip."

"The jerry cans seem the best bet to me."

"Want to come forward, skipper?" he smiled, "You know I did say to Bull he should wake you and let you know what had been arranged."

"Don't worry, I'll deal with Bull. But lead on with the inspection I like what I see."

The middle section of the boat comprised a small but well equipped galley, and a quite spacious lounge with small portholes on both sides from which a ladder led up to the wheel house. Two teak tables with benches were bolted to the deck providing seats for up to a dozen people. Off to the port side was a small chart room containing a short band radio. Further forward there were two cabins for sleeping, one comprised four bunks and the second, smaller one, two. Toward the bow was a small wash room with shower, hand basin and toilet, all of which had expensive fittings.

The wheel house was the only thing that looked out of place and better suited to a fishing boat. But everything looked functional.

"She used to have an armoured bridge here open to the elements, they took it off I guess to save weight, they have reduced her weight quite a bit, man," explained Donald.

"Yes, looks a bit of an after thought."

"Typical of the Greeks" said Donald lowering his voice, "they do a real good job and then spoil it by not finishing it properly."

"Even so, must be expensive to charter?" I asked.

"Well let's go see the Greek and find out."

I had to admit I was beginning to take to Donald the South African, he seemed an open sort of young man, but for the gun I might have started to trust him. But what do they say 'trust no one my friend', not in this game anyway. Honour among thieves, there was none.

We went below and joined the Greek and Bull in the lounge. There, Donald went through the paperwork, not only was I out of my depth but it was pretty obvious Bull was as well.

"There we are, Mike," said Donald, "it's up to you now, £1500 and the Argo is ours for two weeks with full tanks and that includes insurance."

"We will have to go ashore for the travellers cheques and my passport, which no doubt Mr Kepal will want to have a look at," the Greek merely nodded his head in agreement, "and we better ask Joeanna if all's well."

"Do you have to bring her into it?" said Bull, "You're tied to her apron strings? Just sign the documents."

"Yes we do, strange as it might seem, Bull, most of the money belongs to her."

The Greek and Donald were on the way to the deck, I pulled Bull back by the arm, "And another thing while we are on the subject, if it were up to me we would be on the

76

next plane home. She's the best friend you have, you dumb bastard."

Most of this verbal assault was not true but Bull did not know that, it was effective up to a point, his head sank into his shoulders but there was no reply.

"And just to finish, don't do anything else off your own back," he did not answer, "did you understand that?" I said raising my voice.

To which he nodded and started up the ladder to the wheel house and open deck where Kepal and Donald waited.

Joeanna agreed to go ahead rather easily, she appeared not even upset that she had not been told of the arrival of the Argo. In fact, the name Argo seemed oddly to disturb her more than anything.

The rest of the day passed in a frantic blur getting the boat stored for the trip. We estimated the whole operation, even accounting for delays, should take no more than ten days, hopefully less than a week. But we stocked the Argo for the ten days, food and drink was brought with this in mind, the majority of the food was tinned. The Argo was well equipped with charts covering all the areas we needed Cyprus and the Turkish coast to the north of the island.

The villa had been rented for a month, we told the owner we would be away for a few days. It was agreed we would sail the next morning. Our personal luggage was taken on board late in the afternoon apart from overnight things. Donald volunteered to spend the night on board.

Bull had to go into Iraklion to send a wire to his contact buyer of our plans, although time was limited, I felt I should go with him.

"There's still a lot to do," complained Donald when he was told, "you're not much of a ships company, not very good Argonauts. Still I might be better on my own."

"Joeanna will give you a hand," I called after him but he had already left the villa.

I drove the Fiat on the fairly steep climb from the coast toward the central plateau of the Messara surrounded by the White Mountains, some of which still had snow on. During the descent, my attention was quickly taken from the scenery.

"Bull, there's no brakes," I shouted, I was in a cold sweat I don't mind admitting.

"Pump them for Christ sake," said Bull his knuckles turning white as he gripped the seat.

But no amount of pumping helped. A sharp right hand bend loomed fast before us. I swung out to the left, trying to cut across the apex to give us a chance of making it.

"What the hell are you doing," said Bull making a grab for the steering wheel. I pushed him aside and, tyres screaming, we got round with the Fiat rocking violently from side to side.

"Don't do that again," I roared, straightening the car while trying the hand brake gently and changing to a lower gear.

The hand brake slowed us a little and the engine roar increased. There was a short downhill straight to the next blind bend, further ahead the road appeared to level out. But an old Bedford Coach grinding along in low gear appeared at the bend, our way was cut off there was now only one option, to go cross country.

The Fiat rode the ground like a bucking horse. Yet in many ways it was the quickest way to stop us. Large rocks crashed against the chassis and bodywork. A large boulder brought us to a bone jarring halt only twenty or so feet from a steep drop.

"Jackie Stewart's got nothing on you, mate," said Bull who had by now gone very white.

I could do nothing but grin, although I was shaking. Cuts and bruises were our only injuries. The Fiat was a total write off, steam poured from the smashed radiator and the engine gearbox assembly had been pushed back into the car bending the prop shaft like a banana.

The coach had stopped up on the road and people were clambering down the bank toward us. With the twisted body we had to kick the passenger door open and we both climbed out that side. I was soon around the front and after some effort got the bonnet up.

"Jesus Mike, what you doing?" roared Bull with hysterical laughter, "Going to give it a service?"

By this time we had eight or ten people gathered around us more intent in examining the car.

"Ah, thought so," I said, pushing my index finger into the brake fluid reservoir, "dry as a bone."

"So what does that mean?"

"That's a good question. When we picked this car up I checked under the bonnet, it was full then."

"So we had a leak. Let's find a phone and get out of here."

"A leak perhaps or someone drained the fluid by cutting a pipe. I think I'll have a look underneath."

"Forget it, we have company," said Bull pointing up to the road where a police car had pulled up, "come on, we're not supposed to draw attention to ourselves."

It was my turn to laugh out loud, "And wrecking a hire car is OK, then?"

With the police around I could not confirm my suspicion; it would have meant an investigation which was the last thing we wanted. Even so, we had to give a statement at the local station. I said I had tried to avoid a dog which to say the least produced raised eyebrows. It was gone midnight by the time we got back to the villa, although we had already phoned Joeanna who I was surprised to find had already gone to bed. Bull arranged a taxi for tomorrow, there nothing for it, the sailing would have to be delayed a few hours. Bull went off to his room to sleep. While, with a torch I found in the villa, on my hands and knees, I examined the drive outside and found what I was looking for. A pool of brake fluid, or was it oil, and then was it from our hire car? So many questions, my dirty fingers really proved nothing. Perhaps after all it was just a leak, of a poorly maintained hire car, I dismissed it from my mind and after a wash headed for bed.

As I entered our room, Joeanna switched on her bedside lamp. She was sat up in bed with the sheet around her chin.

"Are you alright, Mike?" she asked concerned, examining me with her eyes.

"Yes, just a few bruises, might have a stiff neck tomorrow with whiplash," I sat on the edge of her bed, "the funny thing is I can't get it out of my mind that it was sabotage."

"For what reason?" she said.

"That's it, there doesn't seem to be one. Nobody knows what we are up to, not even Donald."

"I might have a theory about our situation, it's been bothering me about the whole set up, and I know you'll think I'm being stupid."

"Crafty and conniving you might be," she smiled at that, "but stupid, no."

"Well," she hesitated and then seemed to make up her mind, "don't you think it's odd we've got a boat called the Argo, and we are going on an Odyssey after a magic statue. It's all a bit like Jason and the Argonauts after the magic fleece. Half of them never came back, remember those horrible Harpies?"

"We have our own Harpy in Bull. But I don't think I have seen a one-sandalled man. No, I just don't see three thousand year old or however old stories having much to do with us. There must be hundreds of boats in Greek Waters called the Argo."

Joeanna shrugged her shoulders, "Perhaps you're right, but these myths have had the power to survive for thousands of years, that's the whole point. Anyway, I got a small statue of Athena in the tourist shop, Jason used to ask her for help."

"I thought it was Hera? Well never mind, we need all the help we can get. And who knows, she might come in handy."

I wondered why she thought the statue had magic powers, but then it was obvious the people who had worshipped it no doubt believed it had and were we so

80

much more advanced than them. I somehow doubted that. And another thing Aphrodite, Hera, and Athena had never really got on if I remembered my Greek Myths right.

Ten

It was still dark when I was awoken by the taxi Bull was taking to Iraklion. The travel clock said 4:15, it was a good five hour round trip so it would be afternoon before we could set off. I could not get back to sleep so got up and went to make myself an early breakfast. The cicadas were still making their continuous chirping noise; it would take the heat of the day to finish their chorus.

Everything was ready, so there was nothing to do but wait. We took our overnight things out to the Argo; Donald was disappointed at the further delay. Joeanna opted to stay on board while I went ashore to get the day old British Newspapers and to see what they had to say about the situation on Cyprus. Even if it was old news it was still news.

Bull was back by lunch time and ready to go. We had a drink at the taverna before going out to the Argo.

"Bull, that accident still worries me. You don't think anyone from your dark past is after you?"

"Why me?" he said defensively, "You were in the car as well."

That was true they might have been after both of us.

"Could it be the buyer?"

"What for, mate, not a chance, he could not find the statue without us. Look forget it, Mike, it was just an accident. Perhaps some Greek grease monkey forgot to do up a bolt or something. Let's get to the boat and get going we are wasting time, buddy."

With a full crew on board, Donald was soon dancing around the deck taking charge. With the engine running the Argo seemed to come to life. I raised the anchor under our young skipper's directions who insisted on calling me skipper. Bull, however, who seemed in good spirits ashore disappeared below but then he had had an early morning. Joeanna liked the novelty of steering from the wheel house under Donald's direction and appeared to have forgotten her misgivings about the Argo.

It was mid afternoon that the Argo's bows were at last headed for the open sea. We steered due south for about five miles and then came around to an easterly course sailing parallel with the Crete's south coast. Within three hours Crete had disappeared below the western horizon and we were alone. The sea was like glass, visibility cut down to some ten miles by the late afternoon haze. The large diesel's throb was only noise as it gobbled up the miles.

While Donald had the helm, Joeanna and I cooked the evening meal. Omelettes with bacon and mushrooms, followed by tinned fruit with a bottle of white wine cold from the small fridge. We ate it on deck with Donald. Bull was called for the meal but merely grunted turned over and went back to sleep, the fish got his rations that night. My doubts had largely gone now we were at sea. What could happen out here for all Joeanna's forebodings?

The seagoing watch was split between Donald and me. We let Bull rest, he could take his turn tomorrow. Joeanna took over the galley with no complaints which I had half expected; it seemed in the sailing world she knew what she was good at. I took the first watch, eight 'til one, when I would wake Donald for the one 'til six. The heading was still due east with the Argo showing normal navigation lights but we did reduce speed to about seven knots.

Joeanna spent most of the watch with me, but we spoke little. Rather we watched the sun sink astern into the sea, and smelt the dry Sirocco wind blowing from North Africa barely two hundred miles away to the south. Joeanna that night looked quite beautiful; her hair gently blown by the wind, her fine elfin like features and the rise and fall of her breasts might have been alluring if it had not been for all the history between us. However, I tried not to linger on such things watching the Argo's heading.

"We could almost be in another time, or another world," said Joeanna still gazing at the red coloured sea. So it had infected her too, sweeping her doubts away.

"Do they have coffee in this other world?"

"Aye aye sir, right away."

"Oh, and bring up the transistor radio, there might be something on the World Service," I added as an afterthought.

By the time she returned it was dark, but for our own lights. The steaming coffee mugs were comforting to hold. Away from the mountains of Crete the radio was easy to tune to the BBC World Service and in a few moments we listened to the ten o'clock evening news for July 18 from London.

"The coup in Cyprus against President Archbishop Makarios has failed. Sources suggest the coup was backed by the Military Junta in Athens and led by Greek Mainland Officers serving with the Cyprus National Guard. Reaction in the Turkish capital of Ankara was swift, the official government line says this was a blatant attempt by Greece to annex Cyprus, and practically speaking Cyprus is now a province of Greece which breaks the 1960 Zurich agreement of which Turkey was a guarantor. Turkey is now considering her position.

Turkish forces appear at a high state of readiness. Further reports indicate Makarios has left Cyprus and is expected to appear at the United Nations in New York to present his case and ask for further UN aid."

"What do you think of that lot?" said Joeanna turning down the volume on the radio as the programme switched to other world events.

"I expect it all depends what Washington says behind the scenes. Both countries Turkey and Greece are NATO allies. Perhaps the seventh fleet will put to sea and concentrate in the eastern Med and that will be that."

Joeanna went quiet and in a few moments told me she was off to bed, and then did something she had not for a long time, kissed me goodnight.

Of course, I did not wholly agree with the line I had given Joeanna. No way could I see the Turks taking this lying down, but I still felt this would work to our advantage; otherwise I would have turned the Argo around there and then.

Eleven

It had been a long while since I had stood watches and had long ago lost the ability to be fully awake in an instant. Sleep's warm embrace had me and I did not want to wake up.

"Wake up Mike, there's firing outside!"

What firing outside? I could not think, it must be a dream, I felt myself trying to return to sleep. But someone was shaking me hard by the shoulder.

"Mike, wake up please."

I opened my eyes and there stood Joeanna over me.

"What's the matter woman, time for breakfast?"

"Someone's been firing outside."

"What are you talking about? Don't be daft, we're miles from Cyprus."

My mouth felt dry and awful from too much wine the night before. There was only a reading light lit in the cabin, the travel clock told me it was four fifteen and still dark on deck. I had been asleep for barely three hours it was like being back in the Marines being woken for stand to at dawn, then I had the ability to miss a nights sleep altogether, with few side affects but not now. It would soon be dawn there might even be a growing light in the eastern sky.

I was fully awake now and able to comprehend Joeanna.

"I'm sure I heard gunshots."

We listened in silence for fully five minutes. Waves were slapping against the hull, nothing wrong, and nothing amiss, just silence. I was about to tell Joeanna to go back to sleep and stop dreaming. Then it struck me, the silence was amiss, no engine beat.

"Well, there is something wrong, the engines stopped, that's probably what you heard, or perhaps it backfired."

"I knew it."

"Well it's hardly gunfight at OK Corral is it?" I said pulling on my shorts.

Joeanna refused to remain alone and followed me into the lounge, nothing appeared amiss. The galley yawned at us, the dirty coffee cups still in the bowl. Reaching the short ladder to the upper deck, we waited and listened. Again nothing but the sea, if it had not been for the silent engine which was strange I would have bounded up the ladder. What could be waiting up there, one of Joeanna's ancient Greek monsters? We could go and check the other cabin but it had to be either Donald or Bull up there. Probably one of them had fallen asleep and the engine had stopped for some perfectly simple reason. But I was not entirely convinced. Taking a long handled broom from the galley I poked it through the hatch, opening it wider, letting in a grey light.

Crack! Crack! Two pistol shots greeted the broom. They seemed to come from the stern. Both missed but the broom head was blown apart by a short burst from a sub machine gun up forward.

"Bloody hell," I said dropping the remains of the broom, "what the hell's going on up there?" I shouted.

Joeanna's arms were tightly round my waist and she had buried her head in my back. I backed her gently into the galley, where I managed to break her vice like grip.

"I'm going to go through the engine room and see if I can find out what's going on through the aft hatch."

"Not without me you're not."

"Look, you'll be safer here," but in response she shook her head determinedly.   "Well, OK, but let's get armed."

From the galley I took a good sized and fairly sharp carving knife. In this brief period of time there had been no sign of life from the deck.

The most covered way to the deck was via the engine room hatch way and en route I might find out what had happened to the engine. Gingerly, we made our way aft. The engine was still warm, no apparent reason for a breakdown. I picked up a heavy spanner to increase my arms. I indicated to Joeanna the need for silence, she nodded. I took two deep breaths and made my way slowly up the short ladder.

The hatch was hooked back, with the fine hot weather it helped below decks with the ventilation. The hatch formed a barricade and was heavy enough to have been the original armoured hatch. Passing my head above deck level I could look aft in virtual complete safety from anybody up forward. A few feet away was the stern, now completely formed in the early morning light and the sea was sparkling as the light from the rising sun began to strike it, but there was little time or inclination to admire the sunrise.

However, to look forward was a risky business not helped by the rising sun. Whoever was forward would have the sun at their back. Keeping my head as low as possible I took a quick look forward between the corner angle made between the hatch and deck. First to starboard, I could see little forward of the small dinghy that was secured just forward of the engine room hatch on its own mountings, beyond that were the lounge - galley skylight and the wheel house.

Moving position I took a look to port. There, my gaze met the crumpled form of Donald's body; his bare feet were barely inches from my face. He made no movement, blood was running from his body in a thin trickle over the side, he might even be dead, although not from blood loss, there did not seem sufficient for that. I pulled my head back and reached forward with my hand. I could touch his bare foot, it was still warm.

Shaking the foot gained no response. Yet he might still be alive. There was nothing for it, I would have to trust Bull. I was sure no other party was in the picture. I went back down the ladder a rung.

"Joeanna, I'm going to have to go on deck, Donald appears dead or badly injured I can touch him but he's not moving."

"What about Bull, can you trust him?"

"Well he might be wounded or dead as well. But even if he's not he won't shoot me, he needs us he can't do this on his own." I hoped I sounded more convincing than I felt.

I went back up the ladder, "Bull," I shouted at the top of my voice, "I'm back here by the engine room hatch. Looks like Donald's had it. I'm going to come on deck to have a better look." I waited for what seemed ages, but was only really a few seconds.

"Please be careful, Mike," came from Joeanna below.

"OK, but keep your hands where I can see them," came Bull's voice strong and clear.

I got up half expecting to be smashed by a hail of bullets, but none came, I had guessed right. The deck was a shambles. Chunks of wood had been blasted by heavy bullets out of the wheel house and gouged the lovely teak deck.

Bull emerged from the wreckage of the wheel house clutching a Schmeisser MP 40 machine pistol, rate of fire five hundred rounds a minute of nine millimetre ammunition carried in a straight thirty two round magazine, an effective German weapon at close quarters, albeit of World War Two vintage.

Its round sight was levelled at my stomach. All of which caused me enough anxiety, but the look of the man behind the gun made my skin crawl. His eyes appeared to have increased in size and stared, his mouth was like a slit full of yellow teeth, it was as if his skin was stretched taught over his head.

"Is he dead?"

"I don't know. I'll have to move him to find out."

"Stay where you are I will come over and cover you."

Bull moved slowly along the port side, the barrel of the machine pistol laid mid way between me and Donald. I had to let him cool down. He stopped just the other side of the dinghy, by the time he got there he had calmed down a lot and looked almost human again.

"Let's have a look then, Mike, I got you covered," he said waving the barrel of his gun at the still form of Donald.

I could find no pulse at neck or wrist.

"Come on, turn the bastard over. You know he tried to kill me."

I thought of asking how and why but decided to wait.

"I began to smell a rat," continued Bull in his more friendly chatty style, "when you found that gun in his room. That's why I got the heavy artillery here. Used them before, the Jerries know how to make guns better than those bloody Stens and Sterlings we had."

I found it hard to believe at this stage that Bull was rambling on about the merits of German and British sub machine guns. With some effort, and no help from Bull I turned Donald as gently as possible back from the side rail toward the centre of the boat. I have seen enough bodies shot up to know Donald was a mess, he had been hit three times, twice in the chest and once in the stomach, a modern hospital might have been able to save him here he had no chance if he was not dead already. I could detect no breath coming from his mouth. Below his body was a sawn off shot gun.

"Hit him three times, bloody good shooting in the dark," said Bull doing a gleeful little dance, "there see, Mike, the bastard was armed to the teeth, tried to sneak up and kill me."

Bull moved to pick up the shotgun but I beat him to it with a well planted kick that sent the weapon sailing into the air and hitting the sea yards from the boat, I was angry but had to stay in control.

"We had better try and get a doctor or help from somewhere on the radio."

"No good, Mike, the radio's shot to buggery."

"Oh, that's just great. Gunfight at OK Corral and we have lost the radio and the only real sailor among us that's brilliant, just brilliant."

"Well, I don't care he just came after me, got what was coming to him. Must have been him fixed the car."

I had to admit that thought had crossed my mind.

"Why should he try to kill you and not us?"

"Simple, he would have got you two later. It would not have taken much to find the maps; he might have had a look already."

I somehow doubted that one, Bull seemed to have carried them with him all the time but I said nothing.

"And then we would have all ended up food for the fish. Then he could find the lady himself."

"With no buyer."

"He told you himself he'd been smuggling in these parts, he worked with archaeologist, and he could have got rid of her easy, easier than us, perhaps for not such a good price I'll grant you. But it doesn't matter now he's going to be food for fish."

Bull's argument still did not ring true. Alone it would have been hard to recover the lady, if not impossible. No, the little I knew about Donald he was not on such a course, if anything he'd had a marked indifference to our project. But then why had he been armed so heavily, not only with the pistol but he had got a shotgun on board without our knowledge, there was no sign of the pistol so I guessed that had fallen overboard at some stage. All these questions sent me around in circles, there had to have been something between Donald and Bull. Another thought went through my head, if Donald could not complete the operation alone, Bull certainly could not. But there might come a time when he could and Joeanna and I could end up in a watery grave. Or full of nine millimetre bullets.

For Donald there was little I could do, other than cover him with a blanket. The wheel house was a mess. It had been hit by several blasts from the shot gun firing a heavy gauge shot. This rather reinforced Bull's story that Donald had started it coming up behind the wheel house from the engine-room hatch. Although it was a minor miracle Bull had emerged unscathed. For the radio was blasted apart, the main switchboard burnt out and the compass was shattered.

It was fully light by now, I had sent Joeanna to get the blanket first, that now covered Donald, and then at her own suggestion she had gone to the galley to make coffee and breakfast she seemed remarkably cool, thinking of mere domestic things.

Next was to get the Argo underway again. The wheel still responded and the engine was easily started from below although all the throttle settings had to be set from below. With no compass, I got Bull to aim for the rising sun in the east. Donald had said Cyprus was due east, but wasn't it a few degrees north as well? But how far was it, how far had we come? No, I would have to think of that later, get the charts out. Bull appeared quite happy to let me take charge. It even crossed my mind he could be in shock.

The gunfight had cost us some of the reserve fuel. Four of the ten plastic jerry cans stowed on the deck had been punctured and lost most of their contents. When Joeanna brought up some coffee, I sat down and tried to work out our situation.

By a rough estimate we had covered one hundred and fifty miles, that was at an average of ten miles per hour, another twenty four hours at the most and we should reach Cyprus. It struck me that the far eastern coast of Crete was still nearer, perhaps only ten hours if we went faster. The thought was soon dismissed; Bull would never give up having got this close. And even if we went back it would mean the police and time in a Greek prison probably for all of us.

I moved forward to the wheel house, the machine pistol was propped upright against the bulkhead, could I reach it before Bull? No, I was not going to try that, well not at this stage.

"Bull."

"Hi Mike, when's that wife of yours going to finish the breakfast, I'm starving."

"We've lost quite a bit of fuel, still plenty to reach Cyprus as long as we don't miss it and go off sailing round the Med."

"I've got confidence in you, Mike, as a navigator. You got rid of that bastard's body yet?" I shook my head, "Not got the stomach for it? I'll dump him over the side now before he starts to stink in the heat."

Bull even giggled as he went aft but he took the machine pistol with him. There was a splash and that was the end of Donald Temple or whoever he was. Bull came back to the wheel house. None of us bothered to give him any send off, no "when the sea shall give up her dead." It was heartless, Bull did not care, but we, Joeanna and I, should have said something.

"You know that bastard would have done for you and the Mrs."

"I don't think so; he could never have pulled it off alone. No it was something just between you two."

Bull shrugged his shoulders, "That's rubbish. I only knew the man a few weeks."

"Well he knew you," said Joeanna, emerging from the galley with two plates of breakfast on a tray.

Bull seemed calm as if we were discussing day to day things. Perhaps he was telling the truth, perhaps he had not known Donald before.

"What do you mean?" replied Bull.

"I've had more time than Mike to go through his things. He's got newspaper cuttings about Suez and the Marines in 1956, and guess what? You're in one of the pictures, Bull. And that's not all; somebody has drawn a circle around you."

Bull almost choked on some bacon and his shoulders sagged.

"Let's get you some more coffee or would you prefer orange juice? Can't have you choking can we."

"Juice," said Bull red in the face.

"Of course, someone at some time might have mentioned the Lady and who found her," I did not believe my own words but I wanted to give Bull a lifeline. Joeanna was on dangerous ground pushing Bull like this, "you did say he picked you up in a bar, Bull, chances are it was no chance meeting. He was looking for you."

"Yes, that must be it, Mike, him being in the trade so to speak," said Bull grabbing the alibi.

He turned back to the wheel. I brought a single finger to my lips. Joeanna got the message nodded and went below.

"Won't this tub go any faster?" said Bull as I finished my breakfast.

"She will. But this is the best cruising speed, if we go flat out we could run out of fuel before sighting land, but I doubt it. The worst nightmare is we pass Cyprus in the dark. We will have to work on dead reckoning our average speed I reckon we should reach Cyprus tomorrow morning. In fact we will have to slow down tonight. And then there's Donald, do we report him, say he fell overboard or something?"

"Next thing you'll want me owning up I shot him. No·body no case, that's the law."

There was no further argument from me as the machine pistol was lazily pointing at me, with its malevolent round sight like an evil eye.

Twelve

The day crept by under a blistering hot sun with the relentless drone of the diesel engine at slow revs it produced numbing lethargy. All three of us were largely isolated with our thoughts, about which we could do nothing.

Joeanna spent most of the day below deck. Bull was hunched over the wheel in the remains of the wheel house. Me, I sat aft, my back using the engine room cover for support thus I looked forward. I wore my panama hat, a long sleeved shirt and denim trousers as protection against the sun.

Although isolated I did not think much, it was more a state of meditation or denial as if what had happened had not taken place, as if the past could be redeemed. I even dozed much of the time. By the time I started thinking again it was well past noon, the Sirocco wind was blowing quite hard from Africa. I watched a fly feeding on the dried blood Donald had left on the deck; it was congealed between the boat's deck planks. The deck should be scrubbed down but I convinced myself water would be no good, it would dry to quickly until the heat of the day had gone.

The fly, gorged and bloated on the blood, hopped onto my trouser leg. I brushed it aside. Yet then it struck me. What was a fly doing this far from land? Which probably meant we were not that far away either, and then the next question, what land? I climbed stiffly to my feet. My throat was dry and I was hungry again. I made my way forward, Bull was asleep, the wheel lashed on the due east course.

I scanned the horizon with binoculars. What had they told us, in the Corps in all those lectures? At sea level the horizon was thirty miles away, or was that from the bridge of a cruiser? I wished I had paid more attention at the time. Would it be, say, twenty on a small boat, I knew I was guessing and I could make nothing out through the heat haze or sea mist which cut visibility right down to ten or fifteen miles at the most. Perhaps it would be better when it cooled down in the early evening, but darkness worried me.

Below, Joeanna was asleep in her bunk. I climbed in the shower and let the tepid water cascade over me. I brushed my teeth and shaved. With clean underwear I felt a new man ready to take on whatever lay ahead.

In the small galley I soon had sausages sizzling in the pan and a glass of cold wine in my hand from the fridge. I woke Joeanna and took Bull up a hot dog and beer.

"Mate, that looks good," he said with enthusiasm.

Joeanna came to the table; she looked tired and haggard with dark rings under her cat like eyes. But she wolfed down the food and was glad of the wine.

"What a mess," she said, toying with the wine glass intent on studying the liquid, "how are we going to get out of this?"

"Oh, it's not so bad," I replied trying to instil confidence in my voice, "we have plenty of money left and it should not be that difficult to get out of Cyprus."

She took a gulp of her wine, "That's all fine if we want to abandon the lady and more to the point is if that mad man upstairs will let us."

"On deck?" I said, instantly I wished I had not.

"On deck, on the bloody moon what difference does it make? Why don't we kill him, Mike?"

To say I was surprised would be putting it mildly. You live with someone for ten years and you think you know them.

"And what would that make us? No, there must be a better way," I tried to sound as forceful as I could dismissing the idea.

Yet, it was there in the back of my mind it would come to a showdown. I was just trying to avoid the question. And another thing, I was not really ready to give up the quest the lure of wealth was still leading us on, still had us in its grip.

Leaving Joeanna below, I went on deck to tackle Bull on the future. He was still hunched over the wheel, it would be easy to kill him a blow with a heavy object on that bald head. But that machine pistol was never very far from him.

"Bull, do you want a spell on the wheel?"

"No," he answered straight away, just as well I did not try to bludgeon him to death, "I can always lash the wheel," he said stretching his hunched back.

"We can't be too far from land, I saw some flies earlier on," Taking the binoculars I swept the horizon again, "Must be another fifty miles or so, we might make it in daylight, I think you could be right I'm going to speed up the motor."

It was around five in the afternoon we must have had another good five hours of daylight left. I went below and increased the speed to two thirds from half ahead, and then returned to the deck.

"Be a good idea to keep watch," said Bull.

"Yes sure, but what happens when we get there?"

"What the hell do you mean? You know what, we get the lady, meet the Turk and get bloody rich," he grinned.

"And say nothing about Donald?"

"That's right, he's bloody dead. Nobody will find him, and nobody cares. You're not going soft on me, Mike? Forget the bastard."

I had to admit it was unlikely the body would be found, whether anybody cared about Donald well that was another matter.

"Anything else on your mind?" asked Bull in a conciliatory tone.

"The situation on Cyprus, but we won't know that until we get there."

I had answered my own question. Bull turned back to the wheel and gazed ahead while he whistled some tuneless tune through his teeth.

I sat on the aft hatch sweeping the horizon every five minutes with the binoculars. Half an hour later, Joeanna came on deck looking fresh in a clean white blouse and thin white cotton shorts. She used another set of binoculars to scan the horizon concentrating mostly on the north and the east.

Three hours later with the sun sinking behind us Joeanna jumped up, "Mike, over the back, look."

I almost said 'stern' to her but instead swept in that direction, there was no doubt about it the dark outline of land above the sea.

"Come around to port," I shouted to Bull, and scrambled below cutting the throttle back on the engine to quarter speed.

I got a large map of Cyprus from the lounge and laid it on the deck close to the wheelhouse where we could all see it. An hour later by the fading light, we had made out Cape Zevgoni to the east of Episkopi Bay, we had come close to missing the island altogether, the next stop would have been the Lebanon. We brought the Argo close inshore and cut the engine dropping bow and stern anchors.

We decided to wait until daylight. In a few minutes it was dark and quiet without the throb of the engine a few lights winked on shore. But more ominous carried on the still night air was the "thrump, thrump, thrump," of distant artillery.

"We better stand watch," said Bull, "I'll take the first one, you get your heads down could be quite a day tomorrow."

I awoke cramped in my bed with cramp in my foot, funny how I still got it in a foot with bits missing. Joeanna was breathing deeply above me, still asleep. It took me a couple of minutes to realise the cabin was light. So much for Bull waking us, I climbed out and dressed.

The forward hatch I found over and locked, a trip to the stern hatch through the engine room found what I now expected the hatch over and locked. I sat there on the short ladder. So, Bull did not trust us not to abandon ship and make a run for it. But he would be unable to go ahead on his own and would have to trust us at some stage. I went to the forward hatch and listened intently but all I could hear was the lapping of water against the hull. I just hoped he would not be too long, it would get like an oven below deck in a couple of hours when the sun was fully up, which would not help my temper.

Thirteen

It was almost eight before I felt something gently hit the Argo astern and someone climb on to the deck. The forward hatch bolts were thrown back above my head and the hatch opened, with a welcome breath of fresh air Bull climbed down.

"Well, where have you been?"

Bull grinned; he was obviously pleased with himself, "Been ashore on a recca, got us some transport too, an old Austin pick-up off a farmer only cost fifty quid. Had to pay in Sterling though. He was not keen on Cypriot pounds no sir, really got the wind up that feller."

There seemed little point in tackling him on why he locked us up, he would only say it was for our safety or something equally ridiculous.

"What's the situation like?" I asked.

"Quiet here, but we are close to the British Base at Akrotiri."

I got out the map of Cyprus and laid it on the table.

"The farmer said the fighting up north is heavy, and the Turks have been using napalm. But the Greek National Guard," to which he gave a little chuckle, "will throw the Turks back into the sea. Then he had a go at the British Government for not backing the Greeks, bloody cheek if you ask me. After they tried to blow you up Mike."

"Is that coffee I smell?"

I got up and made him a cup. His mood was light I began to wonder if he was light headed through lack of sleep.

"By this map we are practically in the base area."

"Just the ticket," I called to him from the galley, "protected by HM Government. But I don't know we should hang around here too long, might get people in authority sniffing around." Bull was intent on studying the map, as I put down the coffee, "You want some breakfast? I'm making for everyone."

"Hell yes. I'm going to take a shower first though. Where's the Mrs?"

"Sleeping in."

"Good for her, been a bit rough," he finished disappearing toward the shower he called from that direction, "be about ten minutes."

I guessed the Schmeisser MP 40 must still be on deck, there was no sign of it below. As I moved bacon and sausages around the pan with a fork, I considered going on deck to find it but that would bring on a confrontation and a fight to the finish. I might have to kill him, and this was hardly the time or place, I did not know if I could anyway and perhaps it would not be necessary. I had shot at people in anger before but that had been a long time ago and even then I doubt I hit anybody. I was just not that good a shot. Then again, our plan might go smoothly I tried to convince myself this was a real possibility.

Bull was soon back, his bald head still wet from the shower. He was in clean albeit crumpled cloths, and he had shaved. He began devouring the plate of eggs, bacon and sausages I put in front on him.

"You better wake sleeping beauty," he said buttering a thick slice of bread, "this should be the start of one hell of a profitable day."

*

By nine that morning I was motoring westward along the coast road between Episkopi Bay and Paphos, the road cutting through countryside of vineyards and chalk cliffs. The old grey Austin pick up truck, for its age, had a reasonable turn of speed. Albeit the gears crunched on every change when you could find a gear, there being so

101

much slack on the column mounted gear lever, and the brakes pulled viciously, everything rattled, and the truck reeked of goats and stale tobacco.

Vapour trails high in the sky to the north told their own story but here, the roads were deserted and there was little sign of life in the villages I passed. Just west of Paramali I came upon a British checkpoint which marked the perimeter of the UK Sovereign Base Area.

It consisted of a sand bag Sanger topped by a Union Jack Flag and manned by men from a Scottish Regiment with tartan bands on their field caps. One of them stepped out into the road, his SLR Rifle over his shoulder arm held up for me to stop.

He came around to the drivers door as I pulled up another Jock checked the back of the pick-up. My hands felt sweaty and clammy, quite why this was the case I don't know I had done nothing wrong other than not reporting a killing.

"Morning, sir."

"Morning, Corporal," I flashed him a broad smile which brought no response.

"Have you any identification I might see?" continued the dour Scotsman, "and where might you be going ta?"

"Passport do?" which I handed him, "I'm off to Paphos and then back to the boat and get as far away from this island as I can. Seems like the whole world's gone mad."

The Corporal handed back my passport, "Where did you get the vehicle, sir?" he asked no trace of emotion on his face.

I broke into a cold sweat, had Bull stolen the pick-up or even killed the farmer? Surely he would not be so stupid, I tried to keep my voice as friendly and as matter a fact as I could.

"Oh, hired it off a Cyp Farmer, not strictly legal I should think. Doubt it's got a current MOT, or road tax."

The Corporal smiled for the first time, "Do you kin it will make it ta Paphos?" he said shaking his head, "My orders are to advise all British Nationals to stay within the Sovereign Base. But you are free ta go if you wish. I would warn you the EOKA-B have been active in this area against the local Turks, right bunch of thugs they are too."

"And what regiment are you with, Corporal."

"First Royal Scots Guards," he said springing to attention.

"I was out here during the first EOKA troubles in the fifties with the Royal Marines," I did not wish to appear in too much of a hurry to get away.

"Is that a fact, sor," he replied, boredom on the edge of his voice, "just don't pick anybody up and you should be OK."

"Well, thank you Corporal, best get to my boat and away."

The Corporal stood aside and saluted and winced as I crunched the Austin into gear and then took off with a series of lurches as the pick-up was in third gear. I soon got the hang of the gear box and the Austin soon gobbled up the miles along the good flat coast road but my mind was largely at sea with the Argo.

It had been Bull's idea for me to take the pick-up. I was to try and get more petrol for the pick-up and diesel fuel for the Argo we would meet again at the village of Latchi on the north coast. They would bring the Argo into Khrysokhou Bay and anchor near the village where we would expect few questions. After which we would journey up into the mountains toward Ayios Epiphanios and recover the lady. Of course, although it went by unchallenged Bull obviously felt he had to keep us apart. If he had taken the land route it was quite likely he would not have seen us again. But it was by no means certain, for I believe at that stage we were all getting gold fever. Or perhaps as Joeanna had hinted perhaps the ancient Gods were manipulating us. In a way I was glad to be on dry land again able to think on my own.

I soon passed the little bay at Petra tou Romiou, with its two limestone rocks jutting out of the sea, where Aphrodite is said to have risen naked from the foam of the sea. A few miles further west I took a right turn up a prominent hill surrounded by orange groves, within a mile I was at the remains of the Sanctuary of Aphrodite, the place where more than likely the statue had come from.

Climbing from the truck with a pair of binoculars I walked amid the ruins that were largely only foundations with the odd round of Doric Column. It did not take much to imagine tall columns, marble and mosaic floors. I said a little prayer to the Goddess to bless our little enterprise. Strangely, I felt my damaged leg aching, was it some sort of sub-conscious reaction? I scanned the sea to the horizon but there was no sign of the Argo, they might not have set off yet or perhaps would try to keep out of sight of land as they made their way around to the north coast.

"Young man, young man," came the strong cry of an older woman's voice. There was no mistaking the clear, clipped, English accent.

I looked around bewildered, as if trying to decide if she was speaking to me, knowing it had to be me there was no one probably within ten miles of the spot.

She was stumbling through the orange grove not fifty feet away weighed down by an assortment of bags. Her flowered dress was dirty and sweat stained, although it had the benefit of long sleeves and on her head was a wide brimmed straw hat to keep off the worst of the sun under which wispy grey hair had fallen around her shoulders, on her feet were those bloody awful sandals, only the British would wear, that I had worn when a school boy.

"Yes, you," she said as she reached me, "knew you had to be English, no Greek would go sight seeing at a time like this."

There was no way out of it, the words just came out, "Can I help you?"

"Oh, how very kind, yes um, the Greek National Guard have driven me out of my bungalow up at the village," she waved in a vague general direction, "bunch of shysters, I told them they should be up north, not making sport with old ladies, up fighting the Turks. Cowards every one of them. Is that your vehicle? Oh good, perhaps you could give me a lift to British Authority."

And so I had met Miss Vera Irving, who had quickly told me her name and found out mine. I loaded her bags into the back of the pick-up amazed she had managed too carry so much so far, we were soon back on the road to Paphos.

Vera kept up a pretty non-stop barrage of chat for ten minutes or so, how she had been a nurse rising to sister of her own ward, how she had come to live on Cyprus and written a book about the Aphrodite Cult.

"A book about Aphrodite?" I jammed on the brakes.

"Oh my, I did not think you were listening, yes that's right. Funny how men are so obsessed with her, I suppose it's all that love and sex nonsense. I may have got a copy I can let you have in one of my bags."

"It's not me that's interested, but my wife is fascinated by all that ancient Greek stuff."

"She sounds eminently sensible, the Greek Myths, that stuff what a description, Mike, are as relevant today as they were when they were first written down."

I felt like I was back at school and had just been told off and would have to stand in the corner next. But Vera droned on and the fact was I became curious and began paying attention to what she had to say.

"The Aphrodite Cult was not even wiped out by the early aggressive Christian Churches. The Priests of which tried to destroy anything connected with Pagan Gods but they had no hope really. Barely a hundred years ago the peasants round here, on the outskirts of Paphos at Kouklea Village were still calling their church 'Our Lady of Aphrodite'. And young mothers, within my lifetime, having no milk to feed to their babies used to turn to Aphrodite for help. Not the local priest. They would come in secret to the Sanctuary, usually at the dead of night, to the phallic conical stone, very racy like a big penis, and anoint it with olive oil to try and produce milk in their breasts. Until the stone was removed to the Nicosia Museum," she hesitated for a moment, "you know I still think the Priests had something to do with that, you cannot trust them an inch."

"Sounds like you have no time for the Orthodox Church."

"Ha," she laughed, "any church, not just the Orthodox, all meddlesome Priests. Funny thing is was my Father was a vicar, but he was not half as superstitious as this lot, in fact he was quite interested in myths and got me hooked on it as well."

We arrived at a junction and Vera gave me directions. I had to prompt her to get her to return to Aphrodite, "You were saying about the Cult?"

"There, I knew it. Men can't resist her. Even the Turkish Cypriots believe in her and gave her the pretty name of *Dunya Guzeli*, which means as close as I can come 'the World's Lovely'. She was born not far from here, so the Greeks say, from the foam of the sea. The child of Zeus by the nymph Diane, daughter of air and earth, she steeped out of the rock encircled waters where the Graces covered her nakedness," Vera paused for a few moments mopping the perspiration from her face.

"So that's it then?" I prompted again.

"Oh no Mike, there's much more to it than that, especially so if you're after any truth. Before the Olympian Gods, many say an older race of cosmic divinities ruled the world. Of these, the Sky-God Uranus was the son of Mother Earth herself, and his son, the Titan Cranus, took his fathers Kingdom by castrating him. He threw these genitals into the sea and around their white foam grew the goddess Aphrodite.

You see Mike; divinities are not born so simply, all this foam business for Cosmic Beings, what rot. They have grown rather in peoples minds for centuries. They, the archaeologists have found many fertility goddess statues, small ones, in Neolithic tombs with big breasts and heavy hips all over this island. And the Phoenicians brought their earth mother here, Aphrodite's nearest relative if you like here; it was the Achaeans pinched her from the east."

"Who are the Achaeans?" I asked.

"The Greeks dear boy, what Homer called them in the Trojan War."

I was itching to ask her about the statue but decided against it and concentrated on the road again. Vera dozed until we arrived in Paphos. The town was in chaos when we arrived, vehicles jammed the town. The first fuel station where I stopped was deserted. A shop next door was still open selling fruit, the owner told me the garage had sold out of fuel within hours of the Turkish Troops landing. But he gave me directions to a back street place that still had fuel the last he had heard. I gave Vera some oranges as by now the heat was beginning to catch up with her.

"Thank you Mike, I do love oranges," and she was soon sucking on one noisily, with the juice running down her chin while I tried to find this other garage.

The directions were good and I soon found the place like a back street lock up. Here I found the owner a nervous young Greek listening to the British Broadcasting Forces Radio. He was adorned with gold rings on most of his fingers and an expensive watch on his wrist. He was a new breed of Cypriot more interested in money and possessions rather than Union with Greece or years of back breaking work in the fields.

"Have you fuel?" I began.

"Sure some," he smiled, "but not for Cypriot Pounds. Sterling or US dollars."

He charged ten dollars a gallon for petrol and twenty for diesel which he already had in cans. I smelt it which was about all I could do. But he asked no awkward questions. It cost three hundred dollars. His eyes lit up when he saw my wallet bulging with notes.

"I have a nice Mercedes car you can have for a thousand, the old Austin not going to get far," he said making a face.

He helped me load the cans in the back of the pick-up. And then I saw his face tighten and glanced where he was looking. Seven or eight men dressed largely in olive green had entered the street armed with a variety of weapons, their pace quickened as they saw us.

"Get going, English," said the Greek who disappeared back into his lock up.

I needed no telling and jumped into the Austin which thankfully started first time.

"Thieves, robbers, call yourselves soldiers," Vera was out of the car shaking her fist at the GNG men.

They stopped, laughing at the old demented woman, which gave me the time to bundle her back in the Austin and drive away.

"You should have let me give them a piece of my mind."

"Well, I'm sure you could do that, Vera, but somehow I think they might have been more interested in my fuel."

"Ah yes, what a fool I've been, I could have ruined your plans."

Vera went quiet after that which had not been my intention. Somehow we got to the main square where a convoy was parked of coaches escorted by British Army Landrovers flying Union Jacks and one armoured car, plenty of the Royal Scots were helping people into the coaches. I pulled up beside a sergeant.

"This lady wants to go into the base, Sergeant."

"Right oh, sir."

So the sergeant helped Vera with her bags but she insisted in looking through them until she found a copy of her book, well it was a booklet really, "Cyprus and the Aphrodite Cult" by Vera Irving. And then she had to sign it for Joeanna.

"It's really for women Mike, but remember one thing, if you get a strong smell of violets in the air, the cosmic one, Aphrodite, is not far away," then she kissed me and was gone.

"You coming, sir?" said the sergeant, taking a lot of interest in the cans in the back of the Austin.

"No sergeant got to get to my boat up north with this fuel."

"I would advise you to come with us sir. That cargo of yours, well, some people around here might kill for that, or at least rob you."

"Sorry sergeant, people waiting for me."

"OK sir," he said shaking his head, "it's up to you, but let me help you cover it up."

We covered the cans with some old shaking in the back of the pick-up.

"How far you going, sir?" When I told him Lachi he sucked his teeth, "Rather you than me sir, you're heading toward the fighting you ken. Still, good luck, sir," and he turned and walked away.

Fourteen

I took it slowly driving through Paphos. There was not much traffic about. Its ancient harbour, built by Alexander the Great was still full of boats and yachts of various shapes and sizes. I took the main road north, it was hot and dusty and I was hungry, but other than popping a few grapes in my mouth decided against stopping again until I reached Lachi, it was already past three o'clock, I had lost enough time what with Vera and finding fuel. I would still be likely to get there before the Argo but it would give me time to spy out the land look for an advantage. I made a mental list. One, more fuel, two, find out more about the situation up north, three, eat.

North of Paphos the road became quickly deserted. There was no evidence of the GNG or the EOKA-B. The heavy fighting the last I had heard was up around Kyrenia. Still on any rise in the ground I stopped briefly and scanned the ground for any sign of life. The village of Polis was like a ghost town. I stopped in what I took to be the town square. The sorry excuse for shops and houses were deserted and some after a quick nose around had been that way long before this crisis. But some of the walls had been daubed with anti-Turkish slogans, 'Up Enosis', 'Bring back Dighenis'. I laughed at that one, what good would General Grivas the leader of the old EOKA do them now.

Its dilapidation got on my nerves. I got back in the pick-up and headed for Lachi, time was pressing. By late afternoon I had reached Lachi. I parked beside the small harbour whose sunken breakwater had been here since the Athenians had founded the ancient city-state of Marion here in the seventh century BC. The small village yawned

110

back at me. I sat at a deserted taverna and ate the remainder of my fruit.

I explored the kitchen and larder which was empty save for a large carving knife and meat hook that might come in handy. There was nothing to do but wait, I went back outside and dozed in the shade. It was two hours later, I was woken by the steady rhythm of the Argo's big diesel engine.

Bull brought her alongside the small jetty where we tied her up. He was not impressed by the amount of fuel I had obtained.

"Hell, you could still have been looking instead of sitting on your ass."

"There is a bloody war on," I barked back at him and stormed onto the Argo. Below I found relief in a large scotch, Joeanna joined me at least she was glad to see me back. After several large gulps of the spirit I put the glass down.

"How was it with Captain Bligh?" I asked.

"Surprisingly quiet, I stayed out of his way apart from the odd coffee. He had his work cut out sailing the boat, I don't think he'll be able to make it across to Turkey on his own. I had my doubts we would make it here. Did you get any fresh milk ashore? That tinned stuff is awful."

"No, most of the shops were shut or sold out or both, I was damned lucky to get some extra fuel. And then I had to nursemaid an old lady," I told Joeanna about Vera Irving.

"Sounds a determined lady, have you got her book?"

"No, it's out in the pick-up. What was your cruise like?"

"Uneventful, mind you he gave Paphos a wide berth, afraid he might hit something."

She drained her scotch making a grim face. Bull's footsteps on the ladder into the lounge ended our chat.

"Hitting the bottle?" he said sitting beside me. He stank of stale sweat. He helped himself to a large measure from the scotch bottle on the table.

"You could do with that then perhaps you might lighten up."

To my surprise he let the remark pass and I noticed he no longer carried the Schmeisser MP40 everywhere with him.

"We best get something to eat," he said after a good gulp of scotch which he rolled round his mouth before swallowing it.

"Well, I'll second that idea, nothing ashore. The place is deserted."

"Looks like I'm chef again," said Joeanna getting to her feet, "you've had a hard enough day, Mike, how do you want your eggs today?"

"I think there's some steak in the fridge, better have that too, build us up for tomorrow." Joeanna just nodded to Bull's request and disappeared into the galley.

"What's the news ashore?" asked Bull I told him what I had learnt, "Not much to go on other than the Turks are up around Kyrenia."

"Barely fifty miles away and who knows, they might be coming this way, but I doubt it. I think they'll head for Nicosia and Famagusta first, quite large Turkish communities there," Bull nodded in agreement but still bit his lower lip gently in concentration, "but in the immediate future I think they'll stay on the coastal plain," I said pouring three fingers of scotch into my glass, "and build up for twenty four hours. And then there's talk about a UN ceasefire ashore. I reckon we might have a window of opportunity, probably no more than forty-eight hours if that."

I don't know why I was trying so hard to reassure Bull other than my own gold fever was taking over again, but he did seem happier.

"Yes, forty-eight hours. That's enough time, in and out quick."

Bull went off for a shower; I took the opportunity for a check over the boat. I was still looking out for the Schmeisser but found nothing. I brought the diesel cans on board from the pick-up and topped up the main tanks. After which I filled the Austin up with the petrol, which left two or three gallons over in one can, and topped up the engine oil.

Below again I showered, the steaks smelt good, I opened a bottle of wine and wondered whether it was quite such a good idea to drink so much alcohol, and then thought what the hell, would it really make any difference. Live for today and all that.

We all ate in silence and one bottle of wine was not enough. Joeanna and I saw to the dishes after we finished. Back in the lounge, Bull had maps laid out on the table. One map was Wenmouth's the other a large scale one of the western end of the island.

"What do you think we should do, Mike?" he said pointing at the large map.

I did not like him being so friendly but I tried to concentrate on the map wishing I had not drunk quite so much. The original plan had been to bring the boat into Morphou Bay, the next large bay to the east. Then it would have been a relatively short road journey into the foothills of the Troodos Mountains to the area of Ayios Epiphanios, barely ten miles distant. But now the Turks were in Kyrenia, just the other side of Cape Kormakitis, they might even be in Morphou Bay for all we knew. However Bull was still clinging to this plan.

"In and out quick, that's what we need."

"No way, Bull. Morphou Bay is the flank of the Turkish landings. They must watch it, surely you can see that. The Argo's got to stay here."

"We're not giving up," said Bull angrily.

"Who said anything about giving up? But it's no good getting tangled with the Turkish Navy," I said stretching my aching neck.

Bull at last conceded the point with a grunt.

"We have two choices as I see it," they both made no comment so I continued; "it's over the mountains or along the coast road."

Whichever route we took would mean a journey of around one hundred miles. Over the mountains would be arduous for the old pick-up, if it survived the pounding, and for us too. But we were more likely to avoid the Turks, the GNG, the EOKA-B, or for that matter even the UN Troops or anybody else come to that. Or we could risk the much easier coast road where we must run into somebody and have to bluff our way through. By midnight we had reached a compromise plan, we would try the coast road. If challenged we would act foolish lost Brits and if turned back would try and bypass any road block by going inland.

The best part of a bottle of wine and several large scotches kept me awake as did thinking about what the future held. I doubt I got four hours sleep that night and no more than two in a row. Hardly the best preparation for what lay ahead.

Fifteen

By the time I was up I had a thumping headache and my throat and mouth were dry. Though it was still dark, in two hours it would be eighty degrees, in three nudging one hundred and not a breath of wind till late morning or early afternoon unless one of the frequent storms came rolling in from the north. With luck it would be cooler in the mountains.

To make matters worse, Bull was in a good mood, he even cooked breakfast, something he had never done on this trip, but I could not face more eggs, so mine consisted of three aspirins and two cups of coffee. However Bull's good humour soon evaporated when Joeanna made it clear she was not going to stay behind and babysit the Argo.

"It's only forty-eight hours at the most," pleaded Bull, looking to me for support but none of this was my idea, if anything I wanted Joeanna along.

"OK you bastard, and what do I do if you don't return? Sail back to Crete on my own. No sir, at least if I'm with you I can keep an eye on you because quite frankly I don't trust you, and why do you have to carry that damn great gun around everywhere."

"It won't be a picnic with three in that old bone shaker, and a long bloody hot journey for your pretty little butt."

It struck me then if Bull wanted to win an argument with Joeanna he had gone about it all wrong, which suited me just fine.

"I would rather endure the fires of hell than be left behind and that's final," she hissed at Bull, and that was the end of that argument short of Bull locking her aboard the Argo.

We anchored the Argo around a small headland that shielded her from the village and any prying eyes. We put out all three of her anchors, two at the bow and one at the stern, and drew the dinghy well up the small shingle beach after landing. Unless someone made a special journey the boat would not be seen from the land side.

The Austin pick-up burnt engine oil at an alarming rate, I hoped two gallons from the boat's supply would be enough to see us through. We had a spare tyre with little tread on it but with air in it and a large bottle jack. The tyres on the pick-up were in a poor state with bulges and cuts, but again all appeared to be holding air.

Bull brought the Schmeisser MP40 ashore, it was all oiled and cleaned and he had three spare magazines.

"That gun could get us into big trouble, how are you going to explain it away?" I said trying to convince him it was not needed.

"No it won't," Bull sneered, "I will hide it well. And anyway it's a good way to settle any arguments. You just do your grease monkey bit and look after the pick-up."

Before dawn we had set off along the coast road which was deserted, driving without lights. We might have been the only people on earth at the time, our only companions some sea birds wheeling over a flat calm sea. As the sun climbed higher, the sea went through a kaleidoscope of blue greens and the temperature began to rise.

The coastal road ran fairly straight for fifteen miles or so. In the cramped cab we did not speak for some time. I drove, Joeaana sat in the middle. I for one preferred the loneliness of my own thoughts.

"Did either of you read Vera Irving's book?" said Joeanna breaking the silence after twenty minutes or so.

"Who the hell's Vera bloody Irving?" said Bull.

"The old dear I picked up yesterday, I told you about her. Go on then, Joeanna, tell us what she had to say about Aphrodite."

"Oh, most certainly a cult to the Goddess existed on this island for thousands of years. Old Vera even hinted at its continuing existence. The Kinyrid dynasty of Kings on Cyprus had symbolic sex with the Goddess through the temple prostitutes. The sacred prostitutes came from the best families on the island and had to give themselves to a stranger in the temple at least once."

"Not such a bad old life," sniggered Bull.

Joeanna ignored him and continued, "Another legend says these consorts taking Aphrodite, which the prostitutes represented, were then sacrificed to the Goddess. I don't think you'll get off this island alive with that statue."

"You don't believe all that mumbo jumbo do you?" sneered Bull.

"No, not at first. But the more I think about it, yes. A golden statue surviving for thousands of years and you stumble across it, you don't find it hidden in a tomb."

"Perhaps it's cursed," I said trying to take her seriously, "nothing we can do."

"You could try making libations to the Gods. But I think it would be a waste of time. She's got you both, you won't get off this island alive with that statue."

I looked into her eyes and could tell she was serious, I remember thinking perhaps it was all getting to much for her. But she seemed so calm.

"Well, old Vera felt she might still exist, she felt she was a Cosmic Being," I said.

"Not you as well, Mike, what a load of old rubbish," said Bull, which was largely the end of the conversation.

We did not have long to dwell on Joeanna's revelations. Near Pomos we were stopped at a UN checkpoint manned by Finns. A young Lieutenant told us politely we could go no further east along the coast road and advised we return to the south of the island. He told us the fighting had been heavy, the Turkish Air force bombing and using napalm and Turkish warships were shelling Greek positions. The Greeks had been replying with some ancient artillery and mortars. He showed no interest in our identification or in what we might be doing. So we expressed our thanks and turned around.

Three miles back down the road was a fork in the road that led toward the distant rolling Troodos Mountains and our goal but the road surfaces soon got rough and reduced our speed to a crawl. At nine I pulled in and stopped, I doubt we had covered thirty miles.

"What's the matter?" barked Bull.

"My ass is numb and I think we could all do with a drink."

"OK, but only ten minutes."

We had coffee in a flask and plenty of water. My head was feeling better and I felt hungry, I made do with one of the bananas I had picked up yesterday.

Looking at the map spread on the bonnet, it was obvious even without any further delays we would be hard pushed to reach Ayios Epiphonies before late afternoon. When we set off again Bull took the wheel, and it soon became apparent he was trying to make up for lost time.

"She won't stand this treatment," I growled as he wrenched the gear lever around trying to change from third to second and found first instead, making the engine scream its complaint. The Austin bounced up a sharp incline crashing the suspension through some deep, bone-jarring pot holes.

"You'll break a spring or burst a tyre, slow down, Bull. It's not a bloody rally."

We crested the rise, Bull oblivious to my warnings; he floored the accelerator and managed to find top gear. We took two bends now going downhill in a shower of stones; he all but lost the tail once as the rear wheels drifted off the track. It was not the springs or tyres that caught us out. Rather it was there as we came around a blind bend too fast; a large boulder was in the middle of the road. At that speed there was no chance to avoid it and no chance to stop with the poor worn brakes and tyres on the pick-up. It was not that large a boulder, just big enough to go under the Austin and hit the chassis.

After the jarring crash, Bull crunched the gears finding reverse. As soon as he had moved back a few feet I saw the spreading black stain of oil on the sandy background of the track. It was as if the Austin was bleeding to death, losing its life blood. I reached across and switched off the ignition.

I climbed out and opened the bonnet. Bull sat slumped against the wheel in disbelief; Joeanna seemed more interested in the countryside. The sump was crushed and split where the boulder had struck. Even without the engine running, oil was still dripping from the wound. I wriggled under the front of the Austin and cleaned the oil and accumulated grime from the split which was barely an inch long but the drip started again as soon as my hand left the sump.

"Well, anybody got any bright ideas to fill this split on the sump?" I asked still lying there watching the drip which was running faster now. Nobody answered my question.

It was already well toward noon. Away to the east we could hear the thump of artillery and the lighter mortars. Overhead were the vapour trails of aircraft in the clear sky. On closer examination, the sump was in worse shape than at first seemed the case. It had been pulled away from the engine block and was leaking from the front where the crankshaft seal no longer met the sump. But that was not vital, for with the engine running there were no more nasty noises than had been there in the first place, only the persistent oil leak.

I had brought a few tools from the Argo with us and a roll of masking tape. I stood looking at the tools in the small cloth bag hoping for inspiration, but just could not think of anything, the masking tape would never stay there with the oil.

"What about some small wooden wedges hammered into the split? They should swell up with the oil and might reduce the leak enough" said Bull.

"You know Bull that just might work."

There were plenty of pine trees about and kindling on the ground. I cut some fairly thin wedges with a pen knife and gingerly tapped them into place, not wishing to increase the size of the split. But the split ran between two ridges caused by the impact which prevented it getting any longer, so tapping them home made no difference. We ran the engine at idle for five minutes and under gentle revs for another two which produced barely a cup of leaked oil.

"I think if we take it gently, she just might hold," I said.

"And you might get in the black and white minstrels," Joeanna observed pointing at my oil streaked face. Most of it came off with some water-soaked, foul smelling rags found in the back of the pick up.

Bull never apologised for his stupidity in nearly wrecking the Austin, but when we set off again he treated the pick-up gently. The further east we travelled the bigger the pall of smoke in the eastern sky became. By six in the evening we were still several miles from our destination although we had not seen a living soul since the UN soldiers. It was thankfully cooler then as we were a good thousand meters above sea level. Yet still we climbed higher, the sea sparkled clearly in the distance.

Even Bull's gentle driving failed to avoid a puncture with which we lost another half hour. Another puncture and we would be done for and on foot. Tempers were getting short and we were all tired of the cramped cab. We stopped at a deserted forestry hut. A good orientation point as it was clearly marked on the map. In a straight line we were only eight miles from our goal, even by road it was less than twenty.

"Let's crack on," said Bull barely able to contain his excitement.

"Hold on there," I said, "we must think this thing through. There's barely an hour of daylight left and one thing we don't want to do is drive in the dark. With the lights on I don't know how long the battery will last. This old girl has not had its one hundred thousand mile service. This is a good place to stop, shelter and everything."

120

"We can spend a relatively comfortable night here," added Joeanna who had already explored the hut, "there are even gas bottles to heat up the tins of soup."

Bull, to my surprise, nodded his agreement, "You're right we should not go blundering in there in the dark."

Bull and I did a quick reconnaissance. To the north east a column of smoke still hung in the sky but the guns had fallen silent. Through the binoculars we both tried to pick out the plantation a mile south of the village across a sea of succeeding ridges and hills that were dark like the waves of an ocean. But the plantation was in dead ground, impossible to find and we could not even pick out the village in the fading light.

We continued looking for any sign of movement from our vantage point some three hundred meters from the hut and a hundred meters above it on a small knoll. I don't know if it was instinct or plain luck but I looked behind us just as three green clad figures emerged onto the track heading toward the hut.

I grabbed Bull by the shoulder and hissed in his ear, "We have company," pointing back toward the hut.

*

The three men made their way toward the hut but stopped at the Austin. They all carried weapons slung over their shoulders. Two carried what looked like hunting rifles the other a British Sten Gun. They moved with a tired shamble as of a long march.

I heard Bull ease back the cocking mechanism of the Schmeisser as below the three men crossed the crunchy surface of the track.

"Bull, I'll go down and talk to them," I whispered in his ear, "keep me covered and close down the range." He nodded his agreement.

I slid down the reverse side of the knoll keeping it between me and the hut and made my way in dead ground to a gap in the ridge that would lead me back to the hut. Crossing through the trees I came out onto the track. My idea was to approach them openly not like I had been stalking them. So boldly I walked along the track back to the hut making plenty of noise.

They still did not hear me but were intent on examining the pick-up, and all three were smoking I could smell the acrid tang of their tobacco.

"Am I glad to see you," I called out, pretty sure they were Greek and their English would be better than my Greek.

They all turned, the one with the Sten gun unslung his weapon but held it loosely in his hands which probably saved his life, and I knew Bull would have taken first pressure on the trigger of the Schmeisser by now. The other two made no move; one even had his hands in his pockets.

"Kalamatra," they all said in greeting.

"English," said the one with the Sten, "I speak good English."

Joeanna emerged from the hut at the sound of voices, and gave them a nervous smile. I was thankful she made no comment about Bull. They replied to her presence with a sort of bob bow.

Up closer, it was plain they were all older men, not the young hot heads of the EOKA-B, rather some sort of Greek militia or home guard.

"Car no good," I said, "we've come from Kyrenia."

I leaned inside the Austin and touched the starter button. The engine whirred but without the key turned in the ignition, would not start. Their interest in the Austin evaporated with that, and they started asking questions about Kyrenia and the fighting. I merely answered in general terms but added how well the Greeks were doing although heavily outnumbered.

"You should have stayed on the coast road," said the one with the Sten.

"Too many Turks about, and their aircraft shooting up anything that moves. Had to come inland."

They all nodded at the wisdom of this position.

"In the morning I will be able to get her going again," I said patting the Austin's bonnet, "and you?" I indicated their group.

"We head for the coast; thousands of fighters are making their way to stop the murderous Turks."

"Perhaps time for a brandy before you go," said Joeanna.

"Ah, always time for brandy," said Sten gun, who translated it to the other two who cheered up markedly.

So we shared several tots with them, from a bottle of Metaxa, then evoking the blessings of God upon us they carried on along the track heading in the general direction of the sea. I wondered what they could really do against tanks and aircraft using napalm.

When they disappeared from view around a bend, I waved my hand to the ground indicating to Bull he should stay put. I followed the Greeks to the bend; reaching it I could see them clearly by the moonlight well along the track. They appeared to have no interest in us, just as well for them for I was sure Bull would not have hesitated in killing them.

"They're well on their way," I said entering the hut. Bull was already tucking into some soup, Joeanna handed me a bowl.

"Good thing for them," said Bull, "mind you, the Turkish Army will slaughter them easy. They're like Dad's bloody Army. You did alright, Mike, knew you still had it in you."

With people moving about in the mountains and Sten gun saying other fighters were making their way to the coast Bull and I agreed to stand watches. We pulled the Austin well into the trees and covered it with brush so as it would not attract further attention. We had a couple of battery torches but used them sparingly for the same reason.

We agreed to rise before dawn and cover the twenty miles with no stops but tempered with caution. Although tired, I did not sleep well wondering what tomorrow would bring, so close to our goal what would Bull's reaction to any failure would be.

Sixteen

With dawn just lighting the sky, the last leg of our journey began. I drove; it was slow going with no lights. But the whiteness of the track stood out against the blackness of the pine forests and scrub land. Bull appeared a picture of patience, mindlessly stroking the Schmeisser that lay across his lap, as if it were some faithful pet.

Twice we stopped just to listen to the noise of the forest, straining to hear anything that should not be there.

A mile from the burial site, which was still hidden from view, we stopped again. It was now fully light but still cool though promising another hot day. I pulled the pick-up well off the road and hid it as best I could from any prying eyes.

It had already been decided Joeanna would stay with the Austin until we found out all was clear. I had half expected an argument from her but she was well subdued with dark rings under her eyes, she looked as if she had spent as bad a night as I had.

Bull and I went forward in silence. Cresting the rise leading to the plantation, Bull cocked the Schmeisser and made his way forward in a crouch; I thought it was a bit over the top but followed suit, hugging close to the ground. I began to wonder why I was doing this.

The narrow, open-ended valley was familiar which was hardly surprising; we had talked about it so much. But strangely it was familiar from memory too. The picture came back to me of pimply Stevens pointing to the valley, "What about there?"

Yet things do not stay the same, it's a universal law and the valley was not the same. In eighteen years, the plantation, with fast growing black pines so common on Cyprus, was now mature; they could grow where virtually nothing else would. Some of the evergreens rising fifteen or twenty feet, through the plantation ran a track, wide enough for one vehicle and at the top of the track near the closed end of the valley that turned it into a small canyon was a two storey cabin.

"It's got to be empty," muttered Bull through clenched teeth, "after all it must be what with all that's going on."

For a silent five minutes Bull studied the cabin through binoculars, after which he handed them to me. In a few seconds I had them focused for my eyes. The cabin was no forestry building; it was more substantial than that. It had a dozen or so wooden steps leading up to a full width veranda, behind which rose the first floor. An ordinary wooden front door to the right with wide French windows to the left, I could look right into what I guessed was the living room, complete with typical rustic Cypriot pine furniture.

On the upper storey the curtains were drawn. A bad sign surely. On the roof was a TV aerial. I put the binoculars down a moment, had the occupants merely left in a hurry. There was no sign of any vehicle, but the track lead in rear of the cabin, anything parked there was hidden to us. I raised the binoculars again. The cabin was flat roofed, the TV mast was high, it had to be to get any signal up here. I guessed it must be some rich Cypriot's holiday retreat used at weekends to escape the heat of the towns, although it did not look like being owned by someone really affluent.

"It's no good sitting here," said Bull, "let's get down there and start digging."

"Wait, I thought I saw something," I said still studying the cabin with the binoculars. Yes, there was no mistake, someone had opened the curtains on the left window second floor, "Top window left hand side," I said handing Bull the binoculars, "the curtains are now open."

"You sure they were not before?" said Bull adjusting the binoculars to his eyes, "Bastard, you're right. A woman's just come out onto the veranda."

Bull turned over and slid the few feet to the bottom of the crest where he had laid, "Now what?" he said.

I continued to study the house; the woman had gone back inside.

"Well, we can still go have a look. The house is screened by trees, the statue's buried top left hand corner edge of the plantation," Bull said agitated.

"That's right, but they would be bound to hear us. It's not that far away," I slid down to join Bull, "I think we need to get closer. They could well be having breakfast. Come on let's go," I picked up the shovels and climbed to my feet but Bull still sat there.

"No, I got a better idea. You and Joeanna drive up there and distract them, and then I can have a good look around."

"And what am I supposed to tell them?"

"Do I have to think of everything? Use your imagination, I don't care just do it," he said getting to his feet, "the bloody island's been invaded, it's not that hard. The chances could be they will have enough to tell you and they won't suspect much from a man and woman unarmed lost in the mountains. But let's get on with it. The Turk won't wait for ever."

"Why are you in so much of a damned hurry all the time? If the Turk won't wait we'll find somebody else."

He turned on me snarling and spitting, "Just do as your damned told."

It was the frenzy I remembered, the hairs on the back of my head rose. The barrel of the Schmeisser had come around and was pointing at my stomach like a black single eye.

"Is this what happened to the patrol in Port Said? Did they get in your way?" I should have backed off then, I was on dangerous ground. It had been gnawing away in my mind that somehow he had murdered the patrol, but it hardly seemed possible even credible. Even Bull, surely,

126

would not do such a thing. It would have been easy with the Bren gun, last man in the section in all that noise and confusion, "Is that why Donald died? Did he know something?"

"He had a big mouth like you and that Corporal father of his. God, how I hated him."

"Donald was Jan's son?" I sat down stunned, "what an idiot I've been, what a fool."

"Shut it or I'll finish you here."

"No you won't," I said remaining seated, "you need me to help with that damned statue, how many lives has it cost? You'll never get off this island without me. And any shooting will alert whoever it is in that cabin. No, you need me or else your life's been a waste. Eighteen years and seven lives later and you have to rely on me, how you must hate me. I suppose if it was not for that Cyp grenade I would be dead too. But just remember there are scores to be settled, you just watch your back Bull, all the time."

"You've just made an appointment to join the rest, old son. And don't forget that nice wife of yours, I could cut her up nicely."

I climbed to my feet and smiled at him and turned back for the pick-up. I could have tried to circle around creep up on him with a shovel, crush his head like an egg but I would have to be lucky. I think I could have done it in cold blood knowing now what he had done with no more compulsion than crushing an insect, he deserved to die. It had to be him who had pushed Ginger Taff off the cliff as well, that was no accident. But I had to wait, choose my time and place carefully. There was Joeanna to consider. I might not be in love with her any more but I wished her no ill and in a way I had got her into this, well no, she did not have to come, that was down to her. At the back of it was the lure of gold that had tempted both of us.

"Back so soon," said Joeanna.

"Need the pick-up at the plantation," I said a lot more cheerfully than I felt.

I told her what had happened about the people in the cabin, but nothing about the exchange with Bull and his murderous admission.

"So what do we tell these poor unsuspecting people? Perhaps we are from the UN?"

"What in a beat up old pick-up? No, they have their own white vehicles plastered with big letters UN."

"What about reporters? They get everywhere."

"Yes, that will do, we'll be freelance," I said thinking they would carry press cards or something, "but watch Bull, if these people, whoever they might be, get in his way he might just lose control."

"Like he did with Donald?" She said.

We were in the pick-up and I had started the engine which I switched off, and looked across into those cat like clever eyes, "What do you know, Joeanna?"

"Nothing for certain, but if there was ever a murderer, your mad pal fits the bill. Let's just hope everything goes OK."

"We could leave him here, go back to the boat. We have enough money to get back home."

"No," she replied shaking her head determinedly, "it doesn't matter; she won't let us off this island now not until things are resolved. If you would read Vera's book its all there. No, we had better not keep her waiting."

There were a lot of things over the years I had come to dislike about Joeanna, but at that moment I admired her courage, yet had to question her sanity. I started the Austin and crunched it into gear and followed the track into the small valley. I tried to pick out Bull, but he was nowhere to be seen. But he was watching us; the sights of the Schmeisser could be on us at that very moment.

We came to a stop outside the cabin in a cloud of smoke. I quickly opened the bonnet, perhaps if they thought we were in vehicle trouble it might cut down the awkward questions. Given the condition of the pick-up this was not far from the truth.

For me it was as if eighteen years had disappeared. Gracefully down from the veranda came Eleni, there was

128

no doubting it was her, only the briefest hint of grey in her long dark hair suggested the passing of time had affected her.

"The truck's been overheating," said Joeanna as an introduction.

"Eleni, be careful," called a male voice from the side of the house.

But she did not falter, merely calling over her shoulder, "Do not worry Grandfather, they are English."

"How can you tell?" said Joeanna "Are we so obvious?"

"Oh," Eleni shrugged her shoulders, "your accents I suppose," she smiled at Joeanna and turned her gaze onto me. She gave no hint of recognition, but she knew me, and merely said, "I am sorry I know nothing about cars."

"Do you have some engine oil?" I said stammering over the words, "We have damaged the sump and lost a lot."

"Grandfather," she called, turning from me.

Her neck was inches away, I wanted to reach out and touch it to feel that she was real, that she was flesh and blood. Not some ghost from the past, which might disappear again.

"Grandfather, put the gun down before it goes off."

A wizened old man, his skin the colour of dark teak emerged from the side of the house, a shot gun in the safe broken position resting in the crook of his arm.

Dear God, I thought, Bull would have seen him. I half expected a short burst from the Schmeisser cutting him down. Trying not to look suspicious, I positioned myself between them and the cabin in what I hoped would be Bull's line of fire but all remained quiet. Perhaps he was waiting to see just how many people were at the cabin.

Eleni was looking at me as if I were dreaming which made me snap back to the situation while avoiding those questioning eyes.

"I think the old trucks just about had it. We have been looking for fuel, got a motor yacht moored near Lachi.

Have you a telephone or could you give us a lift to the nearest village?"

I felt a heel lying to Eleni, and I could tell by Joeanna's eyes she wondered what I was up to, but all I was trying to do was to get them back into the cabin.

"Yes, we have a telephone but the line is dead. We do have a Jeep. But why come up here looking for fuel? The war is only about twenty miles north of this spot."

"Oh, we are looking for that too. We are reporters," said Joeanna.

"The UN would not let us along the coast road. Tried for a short cut through the mountains, got lost and with the pick-up..." my sentence trailed off.

"We have only a little fuel in the Jeep. Grandfather, do we have oil for the engine?"

The old man was stooping under the open bonnet of the Austin talking to Joeanna. I wanted to drag him away but could think of nothing to say. I could not keep from scanning the plantation. Eleni came to my rescue.

"Some coffee? Perhaps we will be able to think of something."

The old man followed Eleni toward the cabin. Joeanna and I followed along some distance behind.

"She's beautiful," whispered Joeanna, "try to keep your mind on the job or else you will bust out of your trousers, big boy."

Had I been so obvious? I hoped not for Eleni.

On the veranda the old man sat at a table indicating we should do the same. Eleni went into the cabin to fetch the coffee. The old man said nothing but laid his shot gun on the table.

"I am sorry it is only instant," said Eleni returning with the cups, "but our supplies are getting low and it seems we drink it all the time."

"It's just you and your grandfather here then?" I said with an edge in my voice.

I saw Eleni pick up on it right away, her eyes flickered between Joeanna and me. I could tell she felt something wrong other than what we had told her. I could

130

not help think, she must think it odd I had not acknowledged her but the same could be said for her.

"Oh, stop it Mike, you're getting our hosts suspicious. Accept our apologies for being nosey but it's the reporter in him, always asking questions looking for a story."

"Think nothing of it," said Eleni pouring the coffee, "however I doubt my grandfather and I will make the headlines. My brother went yesterday for fuel, we really expect him back today."

She had mentioned no husband; surely it was too much to hope for that she was alone. There was no wedding ring on her finger. I noticed she darted a look at the old man but he was more interested in his obvious dislike of instant coffee.

She hurried on as if she had to explain herself, "This is my Grandfather's cabin, he's afraid the Turks are going to loot it. That's why we are here, a fool's errand really."

"Fight if we have to," said the old man patting the stock of the shot gun.

"There may be a ceasefire today," said Joeanna, "that's what the UN Soldiers told us at the checkpoint yesterday."

"I am sorry; my Grandfather is also bad to live with since he ran out of cigarettes."

"That's one thing we can solve, got some in the truck. They are always good as currency to loosen tongues, you know."

At the truck I opened the passenger door and reached under the dashboard, there was a carton of two hundred Rothmans there which I picked up.

"Psst, psst, Mike, it's me," came the whisper of Bull's voice nearby, "I'm the other side of the truck, how many at the house?"

"Just two, the old man and his granddaughter, but he's got a shot gun. Better leave it to me," I said closing the door, "we don't want any noise; there may be a brother nearby." I turned and went back to the cabin.

"Well, make it quick." I barely heard him as I walked away.

There was no point in delay. The old man could barely contain his pleasure at the cigarettes. The shot gun was soon forgotten as he fumbled with the cellophane wrapping on the Rothmans. The gun lay on its side on the table, broken but with two cartridges still in the twin barrels. In one movement I snatched up the gun and snapped the breech closed. The old man at last had got a cigarette out between his lips but promptly dropped it when his mouth fell open. Joeanna looked surprised but said nothing.

"What is this," began Eleni, "we have nothing, why do you do this, Mike?"

"Now, everyone remain calm, there is nothing to worry about and believe me this is far better than the alternative. Now granddad light up your cigarette and relax. Eleni we don't want any heroics."

By which time Bull had come from the truck up the wooden steps to the veranda, "Well done," he said, "it's a real pity about you."

I unloaded the shot gun and smashed it on a thick hard wood pillar of the cabin. Bull made no comment but had the Schmeisser loosely trained on Eleni and her Grandfather.

"Have a look in the cabin for something to tie these two with," I said to Bull, "I'll get the pick-up around the back away from prying eyes."

When I returned, Eleni and her Grandfather were sat on kitchen tables, their hands tied behind them to the chairs, their mouths taped. I thought that was going too far but said nothing. Joeanna stayed to watch them while Bull and I picked up the shovels and set off down the drive. Halfway down we stopped to consult the map.

Seventeen

It was the old bloodstained map. I now knew how it had got that way when Corporal Wenmouth had carried it. The blood was from shooting him in the back at Port Said. All these thoughts whirled in my head, my blood was up I was fighting mad, but I had to think clearly, several people were relying on me, I had to keep control.

The goat track that had marked the edge of the plantation was now the vehicle track leading to the cabin. Once this became obvious, in so much that it followed the same direction, Bull had his reference point and he became sure of himself. The pine trees were bigger but he was working on some sense, some long remembered memory. At one stage he got down on all fours. Then up again he went a little further. I made no comment but waited as patiently as I could. Presently, he hesitated and retraced half a dozen steps. He seemed to sniff the very air.

"Here, Mike, she's here," he pointed to the ground, his face lit up with joy.

"You sure?" I said wondering if there was any Red Indian back in Bull's past somewhere.

"I would stake my life on it. She's right under our feet."

It did come back to me as we set about digging how long he had hung about, even after the rest of the section had moved off. Perhaps he had marked the spot in some secret way. I remembered waiting for him in the cleft of the two small craggy mountains, like two unequal breasts of some deformed woman that still clearly stood behind the cabin.

Bull lent the Schmeisser against a tree close to him while he dug. We dug carefully as she lay only three feet deep. It took less than ten minutes and I felt something hard obstruct the shovel. I put down the shovel and began working with my fingers. Bull stopped digging and watched me. Presently I uncovered soft yellow metal, part of her lower calf. We had started digging no more than three feet from the centre of the statue. I marvelled at Bull's memory after such a long time. Bull now started digging closer to the head. The gun was closer to me but I was more interested in the statue now. We worked faster, I soon had her hand resting against her right leg uncovered, the hand of Aphrodite.

It was then we heard the crunch of gravel on the track. Through the curtain of pine trees I could see a solitary figure moving. Bull was up like a cat from the ground and in a whirl had collected the Schmeisser and advancing a few feet had taken a firing position down on one knee braced against the trunk of a tree. He was a man used to fire arms.

It was a man moving along the track toward the cabin. It had to be Eleni's brother. I was in a dream until I saw Bull's knuckles whiten on his trigger finger as he began squeezing. Even having put on a couple of stone in eighteen years and not being able to get much purchase from my damaged foot, I still covered the ten feet to Bull from a kneeling position quickly but not quickly enough in this case. A short telling burst left the machine pistol seconds before I crashed into his body in something like a rugby tackle.

I heard the cry from the road to know I had failed. Bull had always been too good a shot to miss from that distance. Why did he have to shoot him? I suppose he was just another complication to Bull he could not afford. But I had little time to consider his position, Bull was fighting mad.

My lunging assault had only driven him to the ground. He was up and on me before I had begun to gain my feet. He caught me a crashing blow on the side of the head with the barrel and sights of the Schmeisser, I reeled, my vision went red as I crashed back to the ground only having managed to get to my knees. He stood over me feet apart and planted a well aimed kick under the ribs driving the air from me. God, he had done this many times before. I was not in the same league, no match for him. I felt sick and a black veil was descending over me, if it did I was dead. I fought for my life forcing the vomit back allowing air into my heaving lungs.

Bull must have been overconfident and too curious to see the result of his shooting. Two more well planted kicks would have finished me off. In his contempt for me as a threat he left himself open. As he rushed past me toward the track I grabbed his ankle and with the little strength I had left pulled, his momentum did the rest, bowling him over. I knew I had to be up first. Drunkenly I was, but could only see from one eye and I was still fighting for breath.

A shovel was my target, the only weapon I could reach, which happily in this case could be quite lethal in hand to hand fighting. But by the time I did I heard the bolt of the Schmeisser being cocked. Would I turn into a hail of nine millimetre bullets? Would that be the end? Nothing happened, at last he was in my vision, and he was fiddling with a stoppage. Like a good soldier he went through the drill, there was no sign of panic in him. Using the shovel like a battleaxe I advanced on him, this time he was not quick enough, I brought it crashing down on him. However, he used the Schmeisser MP40 to parry the blow which reduced the machine pistol to scrap, the rest of the blow scraped his shoulder but there was no force behind it.

"Stop it, stop it," screamed Joeanna.

Her shout broke through my fighting rage, the shovel fell from my grasp and I fell to my knees. Bull was as surprised as I was too see Joeanna standing there with a pistol pointed directly at him and a determined set to her face.

"Make no mistake; I will kill you, you maniac, if you step out of line just once." Keeping her eyes firmly fixèd on Bull she advanced a few steps closer to me, "Mike, Mike, are you alright?"

What a stupid question, I thought. I could only nod. It was as if my voice would not work, my throat was gummed dry. I just had to keep working my Adams Apple a few times to get it going.

"You better watch me damned well," began Bull.

"Or what, you dammed fool?" I said finding my voice at last, "You're going to get the statue back to the boat yourself? Why did you start firing? You have no idea who it was but then you have a habit of shooting people in the back, even your friends."

"I did it on instinct. Who knows, he might have got both of us?"

"Like Donald was going to kill us all?" said Joeanna, "I should put you out of your misery now, but no matter, you haven't got long."

Bull was visibly pulling back from the edge, from a frenzied fighter, to something more akin to a human being, something in its way more dangerous. But there was no time to stand chatting. Eleni's brother Tony had been hit three times in the left leg and hip and was lying in a widening pool of blood.

"God and Mother of Christ," he said through gritted teeth looking up at me as I knelt over him, "I think you look worse than me."

There was even a grin on his face. He probably did not realise yet it was Bull who had shot him. The truth was I felt pretty awful, and may have been suffering from concussion, Bull had given me a hard whack on the head but I brushed it off as nonchalantly as I could with, "Oh, only a few bruises."

I fashioned a tourniquet on his leg from my shirt. After which Joeanna went to get the Jeep and release Eleni and her grandfather and I took the pistol to watch Bull.

Loading Tony into the back of the Jeep he passed out. Eleni said nothing but her look cut into me like ice. And she was right; it was just as much my fault as if I had pulled the trigger. But neither she nor her grandfather used any time for recriminations. Bull and I carried Tony from the Jeep into the cabin.

"On the table," I croaked.

Eleni flew ahead and swept the long wooden table clear, crockery smashing to the floor.

"Boil some water."

I ordered more to keep them occupied while at the same time I washed my face in cold water. Taking a bottle of brandy from the side board I uncorked it and took a deep swallow. I noticed Bull grinning at me in his superior way as if to say, 'And what do you think you're doing?' The neat spirit made me cough but I took some more. My head was thumping, one eye was closed and badly bruised, but from the other I could see clearly now. And the urge to vomit had been chased away by the neat spirit. I had probably done all the wrong things but felt steadier then.

Eleni and Joeanna stood over Tony, talking softly. I found myself thinking, 'Why they are doing that?' he was out cold, not sleeping either, they could have shouted and it would have made no difference.

I released the tourniquet, how did you do it? Five minutes about? Or was it five and ten? I examined the wounds, one bullet had gone clean through the flesh and muscle at the back of the thigh and exited not making too much mess. The other two were lodged further up, one in the buttock and the worst one, just below the hip. I applied the tourniquet again. Both women had stopped talking and, with the grandfather, were looking at me. I was like jelly inside, I had conquered my fear of Bull but now this responsibility was being heaped on me when all I wanted to do was get away. Well, that was not strictly true, there was Eleni and I was sure I would be able to talk her around. Perhaps because I had jumped in to save Tony he was now my responsibility as well.

"The water's boiled," said Joeanna.

"Anybody got any medical knowledge?" I asked.

"Come on Mike, it's like patching up a car," said Joeanna.

"Not quite."

"I am a teacher, my Grandfather was a farmer."

"A farmer?" I said hopefully.

Eleni shook her head, "His hands shake and his eyes are not so good along with his hearing."

"Looks like it's down to me then," I said trying to sound confident.

"Come on Mike, you can do it," said Joeanna trying to raise my confidence.

In the kitchen with Eleni's help I found some suitable knives, needles, cotton and towels. I dropped the knives into the boiling water and scrubbed my hands. I took another long swallow at the brandy, splashed my hands with the spirit liberally and began a closer examination.

"Do you know what you're doing?" asked Joeanna in a whisper "And another thing," she carried on in the same tone, "how do you and Eleni know each other?"

"You can take over any time you like," I snapped, "sorry," I murmured, "all I hope is he does not wake up while I try to stitch him up. And as for the other," I said looking directly at Eleni, "she's the one I should have married, but that's a long story."

Tony, I am glad to say, did not wake up on the table, for it took some rooting about to get the bullet out of his buttock. The one in his hip I did not even try for. After that I stitched him up. Eleni held the flesh of the wounds together for me to close. Her hands were steady and on two occasions she steadied my trembling hands. It was not what you would call a neat job. And the hip wound worried me; I wondered how close the bullet was to the femoral artery. But when I released the tourniquet, the stitches held and there was no sign of further bleeding. But what about internal bleeding, I thought, well there was nothing I could do about that.

Everyone was relieved when it was over. I was shattered, but I knew we could not relax; Tony had lost a lot of blood and needed a hospital fast.

"What we need now is to get him to hospital or a UN checkpoint."

"No pal, your first job is to get the statue into the Jeep."

Bull stood in the doorway with the pistol levelled at us, smiling. I had given it to Joeanna to watch him; she must have put it down while she helped with Tony and forgotten about it.

"He's lost a lot of blood," I said trying to appeal to Bull's better nature which was painfully apparent did not exist.

"You should have left him to die, he's just a Cyp. Now you're going to do the job we came here to do. I've filled the Jeep with the spare cans from the pick-up. Once we have her in the Jeep you can do what you like for these women. Now, the rest of you stay here, anybody comes sticking their nose outside I'll blow it off." To make his point he fired a shot into the sideboard smashing plates and glass.

Both women were clutching each other for support but there was little I could do other than saying hopefully more confidently than I felt, "I will be back."

With a little grunting and straining we got the statue into the back of the Jeep where Bull had several blankets on which to rest her.

"Cover her," he indicated with the barrel of the pistol.

"Well, so long Mike, I think I can manage from here," he laughed out loud.

I was sure he would finish me; he could not surely leave me alive. He had what he wanted. But he got behind the wheel and was gone in a shower of stones. Why had he not killed me? I found it hard to believe as the Jeep disappeared from view in the trees. He had killed so many others, better men than me. I had other things to concern me and made my way at an unsteady run back to the cabin.

Eighteen

The keys were still in the Austin pick-up and the fuel gauge still read a third of a tank. Surely enough to get down to the coast, Bull had taken the maps but Eleni and her grandfather would be, with their local knowledge, better than maps.

Frankly, I was amazed Bull had left us a way out. Strangely, I felt little remorse over him leaving us and the loss of the statue; they had both cost the lives of enough people. But revenge still festered in my mind, and I hoped for another chance to take it out on him, to catch up with him.

"Mike, oh thank God," said Eleni as she opened the cabin door, "I thought he would kill you." Tears had streaked her face; I rather hoped they had been for me.

"Yes, I don't understand, but we must get a move on and get Tony some help."

Grandfather found some engine oil for the pick-up and I topped up the engine then backed it up to the cabin steps. Inside, we roped Tony gently onto a single mattress which we dragged out onto the veranda. Taking a corner each we lifted and half dragged it down the steps into the pick-up. We banged his head on the steps a couple of times which made him groan but he did not wake. Back in the cabin we got together food and plenty of water and sheets to cover him with.

"Mike, Mike," Eleni called urgently from outside.

I could hear the fear in her voice. Bolting outside I found them all gazing down the track toward the end of the valley and the way out, immediately I saw the pall of smoke.

Past them all I ran down the track for a closer look but called, "Get everybody ready to go."

Turning the bend into a more enclosed area of trees I quickly stopped. The woods were on fire right across the valley entrance and although the wind was not strong, what there was, was fanning the flames towards us.

"Bull, you complete bastard, so this is why you didn't finish me off, and were so bloody happy." He must have planned it all along, he would kill us all in the fire saving ammunition is how he would see it. He knew about fires like this on Cyprus. They had occurred during the EOKA troubles often set by the terrorists themselves, they were killers, and several squaddies had died in them.

Racing back to the cabin took my breath away and showed just how the years and being out of condition had told. They all stood around the pick-up waiting for me, by the time I reached them I was fighting for breath.

"What is it, Mike?" said Joeanna.

I made more of regaining my breath than was necessary. It would be impossible to get Tony and Grandfather over the two small craggy mountain outcrops behind the cabin. To each side we were hemmed in by dense stands of pines which would be consumed by the fire, no way out there.

"The woods are on fire. It's almost certain Bull started it."

Several trees were ablaze already, the sound of them burning was like hot fat frying. Then when the pine resin reached a certain temperature they went up with a whoosh like a Giant Roman candle on firework night. The shower of sparks sprang greedily at other trees starting more fires, devouring everything in its path. From where we stood we could already feel the heat.

"Soak some sheets in water. Cover Tony with them and yourselves, we are going to drive out of here," I said with as much confidence as I could muster.

"Through that lot?" said Joeanna shaking her head, "No, we must go over the hills, there is no fire there," she pointed with a trembling hand.

Grandfather took Joeanna's hands in his, "Mike is right, drive through the flames before they get too dense, the head of the fire will be only a few feet wide."

I got them all under the wet sheets and poured plenty over myself, covered the fuel filler cap with a wet rag and wound a wet sheet around the tank as best I could.

The Austin started first time and I took it slowly down the track toward the advancing front of the fire, another pine went up as the resin exploded. Dear God, I hope I'm right, was all I could think. About thirty feet from the fire I could feel my hair and skin beginning to singe and my eyes watering. I wound the windows up. Quickly I glanced behind me they were all under the sheets. Turning back I floored the accelerator.

The pick-up lurched forward and bounded into the dense smoke; I held my breath and stared ahead trying to make out the track. The smoke stung my eyes; soon I would have to close them. Then suddenly, we were into the light. Taking a gulp of air I choked, there was still plenty of smoke about.

Where the track met the mountain road I brought the pick-up to a skidding halt and flung open the door still gasping for air. Everywhere about us was a blackened smoking landscape that the fire had consumed. I seemed unable to control the terror of the suffocating heat.

"Drink Mike, drink," said Eleni appearing before me with a bottle.

I took a gulp from my trembling hands. This started a fit of coughing. She took the bottle from me. "Slowly, slowly," she said while pouring water over my head, and then let me drink from her steady hands lifting the bottle to my lips.

"Is everyone OK?" I asked having at last regained my composure.

"All well thanks to you," said Eleni pouring water down my neck now.

"Good," I nodded. The others, Tony apart, were now out of the back, "where to now?" I said.

"I think I know a short way down, perhaps twenty miles if we take it slowly," she spoke to her grandfather in Greek for a few words, "Yes, Grandfather agrees."

"Lead on," I said, letting her drive.

She drove slowly, quickly gaining the confidence in the old Austin and with skill nursing it along. We drove along for three miles or so the way we had come. Then stopped at a track that turned steeply off right to the north, I got out and looked at it, it did not look promising.

"Are you sure?" I asked.

Again they conversed in Greek. "Grandfather says this is it, steep for a mile then fairly easy going, this way the coast road twenty miles, if we carry on seventy maybe eighty."

There was really no choice, although I could tell by the look Joeanna gave me she did not entirely trust these Greeks. I wanted to shout, don't be stupid I would trust Eleni with my life. But really that was just a feeling and how could I expect Joeanna to share it, so I just turned away from her.

"You OK driving?" I said. Eleni nodded so we all boarded again.

I had to admire her driving again. She took the Austin in low gear gently feeling the surface through the steering and brakes, in effect letting the vehicle find its own way. Her face was set in concentration, once she caught me studying her but merely smiled.

It took us the best part of ten minutes to reach the bottom where we were enclosed in a steep sided gorge akin to a ravine. Here the going was better; obviously it had been used a lot in the past but not the recent past. Twice we had to stop to remove a tree and later a large branch. We had been going an hour or so when there was a loud banging on the roof. Eleni stopped and got out and began a conversation with her grandfather who seemed a little agitated. I checked on Tony who was still unconscious and felt hot to me, far too hot.

"Joeanna, try and keep him cool with some wet cloths," I said squeezing her hand but she just nodded in reply, she looked worn out.

Eleni came and looked at her brother, "How is he?"

"Bleeding has stopped, but a bit hot for my liking."

Eleni pointed to the mountains behind us where a pall of smoke was developing, "That is the fire your friend started in the next valley, we must keep moving. Grandfather says we must go a little faster. Once we cross the river up ahead we should be safe, from the fire anyway and only a few miles from the sea."

"Let's get going then, we need to get Tony looked at by a doctor."

We were soon at the river. This in reality was more like a wadi but for about six feet in the middle where water was still flowing.

"Take her gently across, it's not deep," I said.

Famous last words but it was not deep, perhaps three feet at the most, but one of the rear wheels got wedged between two rocks. All that happened was the rear wheel was spinning on the slippery rock, I took my shoes and socks off and got into the water.

"Come on," I said to Joeanna, "give us a push."

Grandfather already had his shoes off and his trousers rolled up to his bony knees. With the three of us pushing and lifting the Austin easily sprang out. Eleni kept going until she had the pick-up well clear of the wadi. It was hard for the three of us to pick our way across the slippery rocks to the dry ones. With a cry and splash Joeanna went over. I managed to half pick her up half drag her to the bank. Already her left ankle was beginning to swell.

"Can you put any weight on it" I said helping her to her feet.

She let out a groan as she tried. With Eleni on one side and me on the other we got her to the back of the pick-up. Her ankle was well swollen by now, perhaps broken, although I think she would have been in more pain if that had been the case.

144

I loosely bandaged it with a wet, cold rag to try and keep the swelling down and gave her some aspirin. Now we had two casualties. I lay in the back with them and got some sleep while Eleni and her Grandfather rode in front, Eleni driving. But she was unable to nurse the Austin much further, about an hour later I was woken by a crack and lurch to one side; a spring hanger had broken away from the rusty body pushing the wheel onto the body. It was the end of the road for the Austin pick-up.

Nineteen

"It is not far, English, through the wood here about maybe one mile. The going a little difficult, but for you a commando no trouble," Eleni's grandfather drew in the sandy surface of the track, "you come to a ridge line, follow the line west you will see the coast road from the ridge. Perhaps four miles no further." He pointed to the track we had been using with the Austin, "Seven or eight miles this way, you will not make it before dark on the track. With the ridge line, maybe. Eleni, you must go too."

"But no, Grandfather," she protested.

"You must child; you know which track to get back here for the UN soldiers."

Eleni shut up at the old man's logic. We took some full water bottles in a carrier bag. The old man gave me his sunglasses.

"I am in the shade, you need them, English, to protect that eye."

He was right of course my eye was still swollen shut.

We did not have very good footwear for a walk in the hills, I had yachting pumps, while Eleni's shoes looked better for a night out, but as the old man said, "It's only four miles, stick to the ridge line."

Quickly, I looked at Tony, he still felt hot but there was no external bleeding.

"Just get going," said Joeanna when I attempted to look at her ankle, "there's nothing you can do but bring me back one of those Finnish medics. A big blond one, then I won't feel so much of a gooseberry around here."

Eleni and I plunged into the forest which was harder going than the old man had indicated. There was a lot of secondary growth the result perhaps of other recent fires, which often barred our way forcing us to back track around it, or to crush it underfoot and force our way through. Within a few feet into the forest we had lost sight of the track and the Austin pick-up. One good thing was that it was fairly cool although we were soon pestered by flies.

"Hope there are no snakes around," I said trying to make light of the situation and the heavy going.

"With the noise we are making they will be long gone before we get to them," Eleni sounded matter-of-fact.

Stopping, I turned to look at her, for the first time she seemed tired to me and weighed down by the events.

"Come on, let's keep going. We can stop for a rest once we get out of this." She said.

There was irritation in her voice or perhaps it was the claustrophobia of the place was getting to her. Or perhaps it was what I had done to her family.

It took us two hours to get through the wood into open country. We emerged bedraggled. My arms and face were cut and bleeding from brambles and sharp thorns and branches. Eleni was a little better off having followed behind me. But blood was dripping from a cut on her cheek where a branch had caught her. We emerged into the sunshine on the ridge line. Running away to the west to our front appeared a series of terraces long abandoned by the farmers and overgrown. In the distance was the sea sparkling in the afternoon sun as if you could reach out and touch it, the coast road was visible winding its way beside the blue-green water.

We followed the ridge line along sometimes no more than a goat track which seemed at times to take us further away from the sea. The track was made up largely of flinty stones that were hard and sharp on our feet. For well over an hour we followed the ridge, still we got no closer or did we appear to descend, although the ridge had steep descents and ascents reducing us at times to movement on all fours. At a large outcrop of rock we stopped for a drink.

"Surely it would be as easy to climb down through the terraces," she said rubbing her bruised feet. The terraces like large steps going down appeared to offer a tantalizing easier alternative.

"Can't see where they finish, that's the trouble, and your Grandfather did say stick to the ridge."

"These places were farmed once and I can't see any Cypriot wanting to use this goat track to get to them. There must be a path below the terraces; all we have to do is find it."

I knew she was dead beat, as I was, and yes it seemed to offer an easier route. Her grandfather had been adamant "take the ridge line", but all I could see was it stretching away into the distance apparently leading nowhere.

"Come on," said Eleni, "let's give it a try, it's years since Grandfather was up here perhaps his memory is not so good," and she was away already, having climbed down the dry stone wall of the first terrace.

The first few levels were easy going, but further down they were neglected. The walls falling apart the terraces overgrown with brambles then the terraces stopped and we were funnelled into a steep ravine.

"Wait here," I said and scrambled down on all fours using my backside as a brake to a large rock, the other side of which was a seventy foot drop straight down.

Looking to either side there was no way down, it dawned on me making me feel sick we would have to climb all the way back to the ridge. It took me all my effort and breath to scramble back up to Eleni. I lay there panting for several minutes sweat pouring off me. I felt dizzy.

"Take some water, Mike, you're getting dehydrated. There is no way down is there. Dear Mary Mother of Christ, to think I should know better these mountains than Grandfather, what a fool," then she began to sob.

I put my arm around her. "Come on Eleni, we'll make it."

148

"But all the way back through that lot?"

"One terrace at a time, we can do it."

And so we began our climb back. The sun was setting in the west when exhausted; we once again stood on the first terrace. I think every muscle in my body ached and I had blisters on my feet and the burns on my hands were painful. The ridge stretched ahead of us. In less than an hour it would be dark, as far as I could tell we would never get off the ridge before last light.

"I think we better wait here till morning, Eleni."

"But they wait for us, they are relying on us."

"How long is the ridge? We don't know," I said answering my own question, "If one of us slips or falls in the dark we will be no good to them. We are exhausted we must wait for daylight. We must rest."

"It's my fault," she said slumping to the ground.

"If it's anybody's fault it's that bastard Bull, and mine for helping him to come back."

He had tried to kill us all. I made a little vow to myself on that hillside that if we ever met again I would kill him. I encouraged Eleni to drink a little water.

Up on the tree line, I found a little hollow big enough for the both of us where a foot or so of pine needles had made a natural bed. I helped Eleni to the place and we lay down together. I was hungry, had a blinding headache and ached all over and I bet I looked awful. Even Eleni, to be kind, was not at her best. Dusk and night came quickly. Even exhausted sleep did not come easily, there was the sound of the woods around us and it was uncomfortable. But then there was no one I would rather have spent the night with. At last sleep did overtake me, for how long, I don't know.

Twenty

Something made me wake, was it Eleni moving closer to me? Or was it the dream I had? Was a figure moving away from us? I rubbed my eyes and looked again there was nothing there in the shadows. Was it 'Aphrodite of the Whispering Voice'? But I had not read Vera Irving's *'Cyprus and the Aphrodite Cult'*. How did I suddenly know the Goddess was old by the time of the *Iliad* and she had tried to rescue her wounded son Aeneas from the battlefield of that war? How could I pray to her? Yet I whispered the words,

Eternal Aphrodite, of the long tresses, child of Zeus,
On your rainbow-dappled throne,
I beseech you,
Leave me not in sorrow and bitter anguish of soul to suffer,
dear Lady,
But come to me, if ever in the past, at other times, you
hearkened to my songs,
And harnessed the golden chariot, and left your fathers
house and came to me.

I woke again with a start, how long I had been asleep I don't know but it felt like barely minutes. What had woken me again I can't say, perhaps just a noise in the trees or had I just moved position to ease my cramp, it was many years since I had slept on the ground like this. Eleni was gently breathing, her head cradled on her outstretched arm. I climbed stiffly, but was surprised how silently, to my feet.

I could hear some movement in the open glade a few yards from our pine needle bed. As my eyes became accustomed to the darkness the glade appeared pervaded by a bluish light.

Have you ever had the feeling that you have been somewhere before? Or dreamed you have? I don't think I'm psychic or anything like that. But I have had that feeling twice before and these dreams or half remembered snippets of places hit you hard, they make the hairs on the back of my neck stand on end. That's how I felt in that glade, I had been there before, who knows when.

And then I could smell the violets, faintly at first but becoming stronger. And I could hear weeping and I knew it was female. But I could see no one and Eleni had not moved.

"Why do you persecute me?" said the voice softly but clear.

Was it just in my head, or did I actually hear it? I don't know, but felt rooted to the spot. I licked my lips and said, "Who are you?"

"You know who I am," came the voice again, "I am the ancient one condemned to live among you mortals till the end of time. Do not let my image leave this island. Too many have died to protect me. Oh, foolish creatures, it would condemn them to anguish and their people to torment."

All at once I could see a Doric columned Temple overlooking the sea as if I was watching a film but like no other film I had seen before. The Temple was on fire, figures were darting among the columns some with swords and shields. There was blood curdling screams of agony. I could feel the heat from the fire and I could smell it. I had to take a step back.

My attention was drawn to two figures, both women, one taller in white robes stained with red blood, a golden shawl around her shoulders through which the shaft of an arrow protruded from the left shoulder, it was her blood staining the robe. The other female was shorter, not much more than a child dressed in purple. Both were carrying, half dragging away the statue, the same one we had found in the dried river bed. They kept looking back at the temple, the painted figures on the freeze bubbled and blistered in the heat as the paint melted, then the wooden roof of the temple collapsed inward on itself in a shower of sparks from which they ducked as I did.

The girl in purple indicated the arrow, but the one in white shook her head, her long dark hair coming loose around her shoulders, there was something familiar about her. They lifted their burden again and moved off.

"It was their misguided, heroic effort that saved my image. Why are humans so heroic? Now you must stop that image leaving this island. It is covered in blood."

I could hear her clearly in my head as I still watched the burning temple.

"Over yonder," said the voice, "sleeps one of their descendents, poor misguided creatures. You must do what I ask for them and her also. I have no power to make you but I beseech you, as you prayed to me it would be better. Oh, so much better for you if you do this thing. And now I am so tired, so very tired."

Then I was alone, I could hear my watch tick. The image of the Temple had vanished. I looked at the luminous dial of my watch which read five past two. I felt cold and hollow and hungry. Somehow I wanted it or her, whatever it was to return, there were so many questions I wanted to ask. I listened. Not a sound, no movement, no breeze, even if I held my breath, nothing.

I went back to our bed, Eleni was still sleeping. I lay down again and lingered in that half place between awake and dreams, savouring what was to come.

"There's nowhere to hide, Bull," I reassured myself, "for I have a Goddess on my side."

A slight breeze sprang up off the sea. I could smell the salt, it lingered among the trees, was there just the trace of violets? It eased me off to sleep again.

*

I awoke feeling cold, as must have Eleni, for in her sleep she snuggled closer to me. I put my arms around her, she moved closer to me. I could feel her smooth skin was cold. I knew the coldness was the coming of dawn. We would be unable to stay like this long and it would be hard just to get going. I dreaded having to put my shoes on over my blistered feet. My mouth felt dry although the headache had gone but my lips were badly cracked, I licked them trying to moisten them, to speak.

"We will have to move soon, perhaps another ten minutes. It will be the coolest time of the day," I said knowing she was awake.

"Yes, we cannot stop time, or put it back," she said with a sigh, "Joeanna and you, you do not seem..."

"To answer your question, we will split up after this. It's only really this mad scheme of Bull's that has kept us together and both of us lacking an alternative. And you Eleni, did you marry?"

"No, only my work, a lonely museum worker. And now for all I know I may not have a museum to go back to."

"Why did you not keep our date all those years ago, Eleni? I have always wondered."

I felt her body stiffen in my arms but held onto her not wishing the moment to end.

"Let me sit up Mike, and I will tell you," there was tenderness in her voice.

Reluctantly I let her go; we both sat up stretching our stiff bodies and yawning. For a while her dark eyes had that faraway look I remembered so well, then her eyes read my face in the gathering light. She touched my cheek gently with one hand. I merely waited as if I were owed an explanation.

"It was because of my Father,"

"Ah, thought so," I interrupted.

"No, you do not understand," she said putting her fingers to my lips, "that night after we parted, my Father went to church for a service, only a small village church where we lived. I was supposed to go to but they stopped me on the road and held me," she sighed, "they waited, the murdering dogs, until the service was over then gunned him down in the church in front of the congregation."

I gulped, "What EOKA?" Feeling even after all these years, how selfish I had been thinking of my feelings.

"Yes EOKA, the Priest, a weak man, a servant of Satan not God, must have known. What a dog. My father did not suspect me not attending; he probably thought I was with you. They took his body out into the square with a sign around his neck 'Traitor'. My Father a traitor? No, he only loved Cyprus, and now they are doing it again killing Cypriots. Killing each other. I am sorry Mike, in my grief I forgot you. But I always wondered about you."

"My God," was all I could say.

Even then I could picture Nikos Clerides, with those blank, sad eyes he had warned me there was no future in it, no future for Eleni and me, and perhaps he was right then but not now. It was different now.

"You are right to call on the Lord's name, Mike, for they defiled his house. They knew it was the only place they might catch my Father off guard. And now they have betrayed Cyprus again. They took me into the village and kicked me out of the car onto his dear body. You see Mike; even your Bull is not as bad as those murdering dogs." Tears ran down her cheeks and she sighed gently again, "Do you think you could love a museum worker, Mike."

"I'd be willing to try," I kissed her gently on the mouth and the cheeks tasting her tears, "But first we must get to that road."

Twenty-One

We moved along the ridgeline like two cripples. Every bone and muscle seemed to ache and my feet felt as if they were on fire after a few steps. It had brought tears to my eyes merely pulling my shoes on. We drank the rest of our water before we set out. It was apparent if we did not find help of some sort within the first relatively cool two or three hours of the day we would be in serious trouble. It hardly seemed possible, yet within less than an hour we were off the hated ridge line, with its flinty sharp stones that felt like needles, cutting into our feet, down on lower ground the going was much easier and kinder to our feet and we picked up speed.

In another hour we reached the road right beside the sea. Both of us headed for the sea and soaked our blistered feet in the stinging salt water which after the first shock was soothing. I dried Eleni's feet carefully with my shirt to keep the sand out. Then against my protests she did mine using my shirt as well.

"Which way now, east or west?" I asked.

"I think west, Mike, the turning up to the cabin is in that direction."

"Yes, and so is the Argo and Bull."

"Surely, he is gone by now?"

"Somehow I get this feeling he's still here." I did not mention what had happened last night, for in truth I was beginning to wonder had it all been a dream. Or did I imagine it?

We started heading in that direction with the sun at our backs, we still hobbled but I felt much better and Eleni had more spring in her step.

"I just know he's not going to get away."

"You must be careful Mike, especially now we have found each other again."

I smiled at her and we walked hand in hand. Bridging a rise in the ground a few hundred yards in front was a Sanger topped by the UN Flag.

"Oh, thank God," exclaimed Eleni.

"He would have had to come this way. Bull, I mean."

Eleni shook her lovely head, "Maybe, maybe not. But they will be able to tell you."

The Finns were still on duty but the young Lieutenant was not there. It was just a sergeant and three privates. They were quickly onto the radio when Eleni explained the situation diplomatically. She did not say how her brother had been wounded and the Finns took it for granted it was because of the Turkish invasion.

I asked if Bull had been back this way. The sergeant nodded, "Yes, about an hour ago, why did your friend not ask for help?" he said in clipped English.

"We got separated up there, perhaps he thinks we have already gone back to the boat," I lied.

The sergeant shrugged his shoulders, "I told your friend it is unwise to put to sea, there is much Turkish air activity."

But my mind was racing, why only an hour ago had Bull reached this post? The last time I had seen him was at least twenty-four hours before. What on earth had he been doing? But knowing his poor driving all things were possible. The UN soldiers gave us drinks and fruit to help rehydrate us. This gave me time to think, I could see the sergeant was beginning to get edgy about the situation it was his responsibility now with no officer about.

"Perhaps your friend will wait for you, could we contact him by radio?"

"No good Sergeant, thanks all the same, the boat's radio is broken."

"To set out in such condition, at such a time, but," for the first time he smiled, "it is no good being so wise after the pigeon has flown."

I thought his English remarkable; perhaps serving with the UN did that, even if he did get his sayings a bit mixed up. I felt he was warming to us.

"Could one of your men give me a lift down to Lachi and then we can get our Jeep and secure the boat and get Bull."

"This friend of yours, that's a good name, Mr. Bull," he mimicked Bull's large chest by puffing out his own, "as you see, we have only one Jeep, the Lieutenant took one off an hour ago," he clicked his tongue on his teeth, thinking.

I felt like shouting, come on he's getting away, but knew there was no way to hurry him without him smelling a rat.

"OK, but do not be long, the Doctor will be here soon."

Eleni refused to stay with the soldiers and by the look on her face I knew it was useless to argue. But the Sergeant for obvious reasons did not like the idea of both of us going to Lachi.

"Madam, I think someone should stay with us to direct the doctor."

"No," she said defiantly, "they could all be dead by the time he gets here. I will not risk losing Mike as well, and be on my own again at such a time," Eleni was close to tears.

I could see in his ice blue eyes the Sergeant was weakening, and this puzzle he did not want to figure out. The situations between the factions on Cyprus were obviously already getting the better off him. He got up from his camp chair and waved us toward the Jeep.

A young private drove us the few miles along the coast road to Lachi, passing barely a word to us during the journey. So we were left with our thoughts, no words passing between Eleni and me.

Eleni's family Jeep was parked at the beach with the large pebbles. The Argo was still anchored there a hundred yards or so offshore the dinghy was secured to her side but there was no sign of Bull. The soldier showed no interest in staying with us and drove away in a shower of stones back along the coast road. We were on our own again.

"Right," I said trying to sound decisive, "I'll swim out, and you wait here, Eleni."

"Surely, it will be better if we both go out."

It was then, across the bay, we heard the big diesel engine being turned over. But it did not start. Again the engine was turned over with no result.

"Dumb bastard's got the fuel switched off. If he goes on like this he'll flatten the batteries. Wait here Eleni, I'll be OK."

I could see by her expression she did not much like the idea. And was no doubt thinking it would be better if he did flatten the batteries then he could not leave. But she stood impassively, having run out of arguments, willing to remain. I soon had my shoes off and was picking my way gingerly over the large pebbles to the sea. It was surprisingly cold as I lowered myself into it. Not bath-like warm as I seemed to recall it all those years ago.

Twenty-Two

Slowly, I swam toward the Argo keeping my head high out of the water to keep an eye on the deck. The salt water at first made my blisters, scratches and bruises sting, but soon it turned to blessed relief, numbing my aches and pains.

It was not long before a glint from the sun caught the statue that was lying on the aft deck. I had to admire Bull's super human strength and sheer determination to get it into the dinghy and then from there onto the deck of the Argo. But I wondered where he had been held up along the way to now be only this far ahead of us. And held up by what, were the Gods taking a hand? And how much of his strength had he used? But then I was far from the peak of condition.

I remembered the voice during the night, "You must stop that image leaving this island."

I still did not think I would have much chance in a straight fight against Bull. I was treading water for a few seconds trying to think of a plan, but nothing came into my head, all I could do was get onto the Argo.

Reaching the side of the Argo, I listened holding my breath, but could hear nothing but the lap of water against the hull. Was he down below with the engine trying to figure out why it would not start? Surely, he must know about the fuel tap? But he had shown very little interest in the boat.

I moved to the dinghy, untied it and pushed it away toward the shore. I knew Eleni would be watching and she would now enter the water to get the boat. As noiselessly as I could, I clambered onto the deck. My aches and pains instantly returned. But I had to ignore them, mind over matter, "It's only pain, lad," as Sergeant Patterson used to say. Even now I had no plan; I just stood dripping on the deck trying to control my breathing. I looked aft to the statue and was forced to suppress a laugh as it came to me. There she was, not even tied down. I would return her to the sea, that's where Aphrodite was born, from the foam of the sea. I could think of nothing that would upset Bull more. There would be not a chance, even for him, to salvage the statue from the sea. As I turned to make my way aft, a familiar voice broke the silence above the lapping sea.

"Mike, just the feller to get the engine going. Funny how you always turn up like a bad smell."

His voice was flat and calm as if I had never been away or that we had tried to kill each other. I turned, he held a Browning 9mm automatic pistol in his right hand pointed at my stomach, in the other was a sturdy stick on which he leaned. Obviously he had turned an ankle or something like that.

"Have to hand it to you, Mike; never thought you would get out of that fire. Remember all those lads got burnt hunting EOKA in the mountains? That's what gave me the idea. They were clever bastards those terrorists. Did you get all those Cyps and the wife out too? Well, can't stand here chin-wagging; remember you signed on to deliver the Lady. Look lively then, matey," he finished pointing the Browning at the hatch and the engine room.

It was as I thought; the fuel tap was still in the off position. Switched to on, the big diesel started first time. I was hoping the batteries would have been flat but no such luck. But it did give me more time to think. Why, I don't know, but I checked the fuel was clean in the filter bowl. I stood like a zombie, my thoughts back on the island.

Was Bull right? In a way I had to stay and see things through to the end, honour among thieves or some such notion, but there was no honour in cold blooded murder. I owed him nothing. My life was now back on the island. I had stood up to Bull once and survived, albeit battered, to tell the tale. He would not have the statue; it was not ours to take and never had been. And as far as honour went, I owed a debt of honour to the others he had murdered and the people he had tried to murder I could not let him get away.

My chain of thoughts was interrupted then as the engine revs rose and I felt the Argo moving under me, thrusting forward, her bows rising. Bull must have raised the anchor and was now controlling the engine from the wheel house on the simple rope system I had devised.

I had to confront him now. Rather more than that I had to kill him. Once alone and my usefulness gone, he would kill me. He had killed five men he had eaten and slept with and relied on in battle, just shot them in the back. He had done it with no more thought than he might swat a fly. Sergeant Patterson all those years ago had seen the evil streak in him. If I confronted him now while he still needed me it might give me an edge, put a doubt in his mind.

The Argo was gathering speed now, how far had we travelled? How long had I been thinking. I reached forward and closed the main fuel feed tap to the engine and picked up a large spanner as a weapon. There was not much time, a few more revolutions and the engine would splutter and cough to a stop, seconds only to use the fuel in the lines. I made my way to the short ladder leading up to the aft hatch. What was he up to? The engine coughed and stopped, then picked up again, stopped again, silence. I had expected him to come down here. I wanted him to, but I could not wait I must force the issue.

On deck he was stood beside the wheel house gazing out to sea toward the north-east at something low on the horizon, barely visible against the glare of the sun. The sun's rays caught the object sending a flash of silvery light toward the land. It dawned on me what it was.

"It's a plane," I said, "any aircraft on this coast will be Turkish," I barked rushing to the wheel house, snatching up the binoculars there.

"Don't try that one with me, creeping around with a dirty great spanner. And the engine stopped again," he laughed, "bloody plane's not interested in us. What, do you think I'm a kid you can frighten with a 'look behind you'?"

How wrong he was. It was a Phantom Jet of the Turkish Air Force alone on patrol or perhaps using this route to check on the flank of his countrymen's ground forces, before turning north back home to the Turkish mainland after his bombing run against the Greeks. He would be on us in two or three minutes if he did not turn away now. Under the body, the Phantom had cannon like a gattling gun; it could fire hundreds of shells a minute, more than enough to deal with us.

And there we were, a sitting duck, dead in the water in a boat that had the sleek lines of a patrol boat and worse than that still, with the Greek flag fluttering limply from the stern. We had two chances; he might be low on fuel and think us not worth the effort. Or he might not have seen us yet against the coast, and now with the engine stopped there was no tell-tale white wake to show up on the blue sea. But both were long shots. The Phantom carried a two man crew, pilot and observer. The shore was only half a mile away, and then it struck me. I dropped the glasses and started hobbling aft as quickly as I could, waving my arms frantically and shouting. The latter was ridiculous, the crew could never have heard me, but I knew then the avenging angel was coming.

"Come back here," yelled Bull.

I heard the crack from his pistol once, twice. One bullet whistled past my head. I took a last look; the Phantom was much closer now and much bigger like a menacing bird of prey closing on us at 500 miles per hour, the red sickle moons were clearly marked on the wings. They must have seen us by now.

"Come on, my beauty," I cried, and waited no longer but dived over the side.

Deliberately, I kept my momentum going down. Not until my lungs were bursting did I turn toward the surface and broke it, gasping for air but ready to dive again.

The Phantom passed my head with feet to spare; it had swept past the Argo and racked the plywood hull with cannon shells. She was already down by the stern and listing to port. Flames were licking from the engine room hatchway and at any time might engulf the entire craft. Had the Argo still used petrol engines she would probably have exploded straight away. The Phantom made a sharp turn and was coming back.

Bull was on deck; he had the statue and was struggling to drop her over the side. He looked so pathetic. It must have been then he noticed the Phantom coming back. He dropped to one knee with the pistol and started firing. One short burst from the Phantom's cannons and it was all over. With a whoosh, the Argo exploded into a million plywood fragments upwards and outwards. I was safely far enough away. But I never saw Bull again, yet strangely I did the statue.

It was as if she did a cartwheel from the deck, the sun caught her golden body and sent streaks of yellow light racing across the sea. And then, as if in slow motion, she entered the water feet first, only feet from where I was treading water, creating a small wash of foam as she entered the water. The face looked at me before it disappeared, fixing me with her cold metallic stare and then she had gone below the surface.

The Phantom cleared the pall of smoke and turned to the north. Within minutes it was as if the Argo, the Phantom Jet, and the statue had never existed.

I turned toward the shore. I don't know if it was a trick of the light but the golden rays from the statue pointed on the surface of the sea straight toward the dinghy coming toward me with Eleni at the helm. She stood up and waved, I waved back, she had clearly spotted me. A gust of wind caught her long dark hair, she smoothed it back letting it fall in a cascade over her left shoulder, and at last the golden rays on the surface of the sea disappeared.

Cyprus

The events in this book are purely fiction. The Republic of Cyprus came into being on 16 August 1960 thus ending some eighty years of British Rule. However, the island was not partitioned as the Turkish Cypriots had wanted after independence. The future of the Turkish minority was safeguarded in the new parliament with the power of veto on issues of security and external policy. The Treaty of Zurich was a tripartite agreement between Britain, Turkey, and Greece creating an independent Cyprus whose sovereignty was guaranteed by these powers, while at the same time Britain retained sovereign rights in respect of her two military bases of Akrotiri and Dhekelia.

In 1964, because of wide spread violence and intimidation between the two communities, and a Turkish treaty of intervention, the United Nations sent a peace keeping force to the island.

For a decade Cyprus progressed economically, her tourist trade booming, while remaining politically, highly unstable. The movements of Turks were restricted and they suffered economic blockades for refusing to recognise the authority of the Cypriot Government who were mostly Greek Cypriots. The Turkish Cypriots retaliated by keeping the Greeks out of their enclaves.

Direct interference by Athens in Cypriot affairs, in the form of a coup against President Arch Bishop Makarios compelled Turkey to take aggressive action in July 1974 or risk ENOSIS Union with Greece. They invaded, occupying the northern part of the island. Claiming as a guarantor power they had the right to protect the threatened Turkish Cypriot minority. Britain, as another guarantor, took no effective steps to interfere, but did reinforce her own bases by land and sea, and was mainly responsible for evacuating thousands of foreign nationals on holiday and helping Greek or Turkish Cypriot civilians caught up in the fighting. Under pressure from the USA and other NATO members Greece was deterred from taking military action and the Greek Government of the Colonels fell as a result.

The invasion has meant the displacement of 210,000 people, 180,000 of whom were Greek Cypriots, and on whose land the Turkish Cypriots were later settled. It seems, thirty years on, Cyprus will remain a divided land. Even thought the UN has tried hard over the years to find a solution, even the lure of a United Cyprus within the European Community could not overcome the intransigence of some politicians. However, both sides were forced by the EU Commissioners to put a UN Plan for a federated Cyprus before the peoples of the island. Thus the people, both north and south, had the chance on the 24 April 2004 to vote for the UN Plan and put history behind them, before the south was due to join the EU on 1 May.

76% in the Greek Cypriot South voted against the plan put forward by Kofi Annan, the UN Secretary-General, which had been backed by the EU and the United States. While people in the Turkish Cypriot North voted 64% in favour. Perhaps the EU should have insisted only a united Cyprus could join the EU, thus both sides would have had something to gain.

Today the people of Cyprus have worked hard to repair the damage of war and in the South, and to a lesser extent in the North; the tourist trade has grown to become a major industry. But the wounds inflicted on people forced to leave their homes will not be so easy to heal, and are in a way just another chapter in the four hundred year history of hatred between Greek and Turk, Moslem and Christian. Now the EU has also become embroiled in the Cypriot labyrinth.

National Service

From 1945 until 1963, National Service existed within the armed forces of Britain. Some two million men went through the system. Originally under the National Service Bill enlistment was for 18 months, later reduced to 12 months and then again extended to 18 months and in 1950, two years became the term. These young men, mostly eighteen-year-olds saw active service in many parts of the world with the UN and as Britain retreated from her Empire.

Most who entered the Royal Marines had chosen to serve in a unit which offered a physical challenge, a disciplined existence. Entry was by no means easy and conscripts entering the Corps were to a certain extent "volunteers" and already by the nature of the selection process ideal raw material to produce Marines worthy of comparison with their regular counterparts. Few NS men were found above the rank of Marine for those in charge, NCOs and Officers, were veterans of campaigns from the Second World War, the Canal Zone, the Jungles of Malaya and the Korean War. Also everyone in the Corps was treated the same, regular or NS.

During operations against EOKA in June 1956, several British Soldiers lost their lives in forest fires, mainly from the Gordon Highlanders and the Royal Norfolk Regiment, it is unclear to this day if the fires were started by a deliberate act or were the result of an accident.

Glossary of Terms

Albion	Roman Term for Britain.
AWOL	Absent without leave.
Bren Gun	.303 British Medium Machine Gun
Buzz	Rumour based on fact.
Dogwatch	Either of two watches on ships, four to six or six to eight pm.
EOKA	National Organisation of Cypriot Fighters
EOKA-B	Second version of above relating to 1974.
ENOSIS	Union with Greece for Cyprus.
Fred Karno's Army	Slovenly soldiers.
The Gut	Strait Street Valletta Malta.
GNG	Greek National Guard, type of Home Guard.

Janner	Person from the West Country of England, Devon.
NATO	North Atlantic Treaty Organisation.
Oppo	Royal Marine slang for friend or buddy.
Pussers	Royal Navy & Royal Marine slang for issued kit.
Recca	Reconnaissance mission.
RM	Royal Marines.
RAF	Royal Air Force.
SBA's	British Sovereign Base Areas on Cyprus.
Schmisser MP40	German 9mm sub machine gun of WWII vintage.
SLR	Self Loading Rifle 7.62.
Sprongs	Royal Marine slang for inexperienced Marine.
Squaddies	Term for Private Soldiers in the British Army.
Sten Gun	British 9mm sub machine gun of

	WWII vintage.
Sterling Gun	Similar to above but updated.
UN	United Nations.
Wadi	Dried up river bed.
Yarn	Story or tale.
Yomp	Royal Marine slang for long march with full equipment.

Printed in the United Kingdom by
Lightning Source UK Ltd., Milton Keynes
140640UK00001B/34/A